YORK NOTES

General Editors: Professor A.N. Jeffares (*University of Stirling*) & Professor Suheil Bushrui (*American University of Beirut*)

Thomas Hardy

FAR FROM THE MADDING CROWD

Notes by Barbara Murray

MA B PHIL (ST ANDREWS) PH D (CAMBRIDGE)
Lecturer in English, University of St Andrews

YORK PRESS
Immeuble Esseily, Place Riad Solh, Beirut.

LONGMAN GROUP LIMITED
Longman House, Burnt Mill, Harlow,
Essex CM20 2JE, England
Associated companies, branches and representatives
throughout the world

First published 1982
Eleventh impression 1994

ISBN 0-582-78296-1

Produced by Longman Singapore Publishers Pte Ltd
Printed in Singapore

Contents

Part 1

Introduction

Far from the madding crowd's ignoble strife
Their sober wishes never learn'd to stray;
Along the cool, sequester'd vale of life
They kept the noiseless tenor of their way.
                    Thomas Gray: 'Elegy in a Country Churchyard', 1750.

Thomas Hardy's life

In August 1871 Hardy sent to the publishing house of Macmillan the manuscript of *Under the Greenwood Tree*. In writing this 'story of rural life' Hardy says that he was prompted by reviews of his earlier, less successful works; 'they indicate powers that might, and ought, to be extended largely in that direction' (unsigned review, *Spectator*, 22 April 1871, pp. 481–3). In most of his following novels Hardy was to accept this insight into his special power and to adopt as a setting that portion of south-west England with which he was most familiar. In *Far from the Madding Crowd* this is, for the first time, referred to as 'Wessex'. In this rural setting, 'far from the madding crowd', Hardy was, ironically, to examine all sorts of 'noble [and ignoble] strife' and to reveal that the countryman's surroundings are not necessarily 'cool, sequester'd' and that his inner life may be by no means 'noiseless'. He was particularly fitted for this task by his birth and upbringing.

Thomas Hardy was born in the village of Higher Bockhampton in Dorset on 2 June 1840. His father was a builder and mason, and his mother, albeit a former serving-maid, was a well-read woman of strong personality and intelligence. From an early age this impressionable country boy was both surrounded by the traditional aspects of rural life – with its superstitions, folklore, culture and pastimes – and given an education, first in Bockhampton, then in Dorchester, which was the basis for his further self-education. In 1856 he was articled to a Dorchester architect but continued his studies with the guidance and advice of Horace Moule, the son of a neighbouring parish rector. Moule was a classical scholar, eight years Hardy's senior, whose friendship Hardy greatly valued, and whose suicide in Cambridge in 1873 may have affected the tone of *Far from the Madding Crowd*, which Hardy was writing at the time.

In 1862 Hardy went to London as an assistant in an architect's office.

T

In London he attended plays, frequented art galleries, and continued his reading of contemporary English writers, notably T. H. Huxley (1825–95), Algernon Swinburne (1837–1901), and Robert Browning (1812–89). By 1867 he was writing poetry, although none of this early work achieved publication. He then returned to Dorset and continued his work as an architect while composing his first two novels (the first, *The Poor Man and the Lady*, was never published). While working as an architect in Cornwall in 1870 he met Emma Gifford, whom he married in 1874, the year of the publication of *Far from the Madding Crowd*. This was his fourth published novel and it established his name as a writer. Emma encouraged his writing and, with his increasing popularity and success, he was now able to abandon his career as an architect.

During the next ten years Hardy and his wife travelled in Britain and abroad and moved house several times within the Wessex area. For a short spell (1878–81) they lived on the outskirts of London and throughout the period they returned to the city for several months of nearly every year. With Hardy's increasing fame the range of their friends widened to include distinguished men of letters, including Alfred, Lord Tennyson (1809–92) and Robert Browning. It was not until 1885 that they finally settled at Max Gate, the house Hardy had designed for them just outside Dorchester.

The next ten years saw the publication of Hardy's greatest novels: *The Mayor of Casterbridge* (begun in 1884), *The Woodlanders, Tess of the d'Urbervilles* (this was planned as early as 1888), and *Jude the Obscure* (initiated in 1892), as well as several collections of short stories. Hardy and his wife continued to travel, making visits to Italy and France as well as London and Dublin, but a rift was clearly developing between them. It has been suggested that Emma had inherited a streak of insanity. It is by no means clear that this was so, although she did become increasingly obsessed with her husband's social inferiority. Matters were not helped by the damning reception of *Jude* in 1896 ('There may be books more disgusting, more impious as regards human nature, more foul in detail ... but not ... from any Master's hand', *Blackwood's Magazine*, January 1896, clix, 135–49). After this Hardy gave up novel-writing (*The Well-Beloved*, published in 1897, had been written ten years earlier) and devoted himself to the preparation of his epic drama, *The Dynasts*, and to the composition of poetry, of which the first volume, *Wessex Poems*, appeared in 1898. *The Dynasts* was published between 1904 and 1908 and the third collection of poetry in 1909. For all the notoriety of *Jude*, Hardy was increasingly heaped with honours; in the first years of the new century he received an honorary degree (1905), the Order of Merit (1910), and the Gold Medal of the Royal Society of Literature (1912). In 1912 his wife died and the discovery of her notebook of reminiscences awoke a spirit of remorse, grief and sorrow in Hardy. He revisited

Cornwall in the following year and in this period composed at least fifty poems concerning Emma.

In 1914 he married his housekeeper and secretary, Florence Dugdale, and it was with her aid that he began to prepare his autobiography (presented as if written by her and published in 1928) and destroyed his old notebooks and private papers. He continued to write poetry, producing eight volumes in all; and in 1927, at the age of eighty-seven, was asked to lay the foundation-stone of the new Dorchester Grammar School. He died at Max Gate on 11 January 1928 and his ashes were laid in the Poets' Corner of Westminster Abbey in London. His heart, however, was buried in Emma's grave at Stinsford, near the tombs of his family and in the deep tranquillity of a Wessex churchyard.

The early 1870s

A brief look at Hardy's activities and interests in the year or so before publication of *Far from the Madding Crowd* in 1874 will give some idea of the spirit in which it was conceived; its publication both coincided with, and contributed to, a turn in Hardy's fortunes.

After setbacks (with the rejection of *The Poor Man* in 1868) and adverse criticism (*Desperate Remedies* of 1871 was considered to be over-complicated) Hardy had achieved some success with *Under the Greenwood Tree* (1872) and *A Pair of Blue Eyes* (1873). In fact Leslie Stephen (1832–1904), editor of *The Cornhill Magazine*, was so pleased with the former that he wrote to Hardy in 1872 indicating that he would be happy to make use of further work by the young author. Hardy replied that he had a pastoral tale in mind, gave its title, and said that the main characters would probably be a young woman-farmer (Hardy may have known of Catherine Hawkins who managed her own farm near Weymouth), a shepherd, and a sergeant of cavalry. Stephen received the first dozen chapters on 1 October 1873 and was so pleased with them that he suggested publication should begin in January.

This success imparted confidence to Hardy in adopting his new career, but other events occurred in these years which also contributed to his sense of purpose. The suicide of Horace Moule in September 1873 was a culmination of years of increasing depression. It was a terrible shock to Hardy but it roughly coincided with the advent of Leslie Stephen as perhaps a more constructive literary mentor. Stephen advised the removal of several superfluous scenes from *Far from the Madding Crowd*, including one for the bailiff, Pennyways, and an episode concerning foot-rot in sheep as a source of miscalculated confrontation between Troy and Oak.

While Emma Gifford had been a source of much support and material aid in the preparation, particularly, of *Desperate Remedies* in the autumn of 1870, Hardy saw little of her in the autumn of 1873 while he was writing *Far from the Madding Crowd* (although it was partly owing to its success that they were able to be married in the following September). Instead Hardy composed the novel, which was finished in July 1874, at home in Dorset among the sort of people about whom he was writing. They were the models for his characters as he created the neighbourhood of Weatherbury; and it is possibly his mother's influence which affected his view of the marriageable female and imparted the stock of folk-wisdom and country superstition on which he drew. Always praised for the accuracy of his rural descriptions, Hardy was able to re-create the true flavour of country life because he had come from it and lived with it.

Social background

In the Preface accompanying a later edition of the novel (1895) Hardy speaks of the 'recent supplanting of the class of stationary cottagers, who carried on the local traditions and humours, by a population of more or less migratory labourers'. This novel is set in the golden period which preceded the disruption of rural activities and customs in the last decades of the nineteenth century. Hardy speaks of the movement of labour; in later novels he was to depict the havoc which mechanisation could wreak within individual lives.

In *Far from the Madding Crowd*, however, the process has not begun. Cows are milked, sheep are shorn, hay is cut, and ricks are thatched in the ancient manner with knowledge passed on from generation to generation within a more or less stable population. Hardy celebrates the value of these occupations in celebrating the timelessness of the old barn (Chapter 22). Unlike the castle or church, altered as politics or religion change, the barn is a monument to the sanctity of work; 'the defence and salvation of the body by daily bread is still a study, a religion, and a desire'. How disturbing the effect of change will be to these people is made clear in Chapter 15. For them the uprooting of a tree marks 'stirring times', and the alteration of a well to a pump is to be contemplated with some awe; 'what we live to see nowadays!'

Here, where the eviction of tenants holding a property only for life has not yet created unsettlement and division, and where mechanisation has not yet caused unemployment nor put a new heartlessness into work, there is employment for all, which ensures both continuity and co-operation. Poorgrass is the carter, but he helps out with other jobs; the Miller girls have a variety of useful work which is their province (Chapter 10). But not all were such generous employers as Bathsheba. The maltster recounts how 'Old Twills' employed him for eleven months only. A full year's employment would have qualified him for parish charity should he have become disabled. How depressing the situation could be is outlined at the hiring fair in Chapter 6. A man as able as Oak offers himself to the scrutiny of prospective employers, like a horse in a market; and, finding no takers, is forced to move on.

The nadir to which circumstances could drive the poor is illustrated in the fate of Fanny Robin. The Poor Laws stipulated that each parish should provide for its own destitutes. A number of parishes would combine under one Board of Guardians to administer these laws, erecting a Union Workhouse paid for from the parish rates. These workhouses were regarded with dread by those most threatened with needing them, conditions being almost inhumanly harsh. In fact Hardy uses metaphors of death in describing the Casterbridge Union; it is so sparsely made that poverty shows through it 'as the shape of a body is visible under a winding-sheet' (Chapter 40). He also makes social comment as he draws a stark contrast between the rich and the poor and the former's ignorance of the real conditions of the latter: 'A neighbouring earl once said that he would give up a year's rental to have at his own door the view enjoyed by the inmates from theirs – and very probably the inmates would have given up the view for his year's rental'. But by and large such comment does not obtrude, and in this particular novel Hardy is not gloomily reviewing the lot of the individual who is in despairing conflict with the conditions and *mores* of his society.

A note on the text

Far from the Madding Crowd was first published in serial form in *The Cornhill Magazine*, beginning in January 1874. It was published in book form by Smith, Elder & Co., London, in November 1874, appearing in two volumes in an edition of one thousand. A second impression, revised, was made in 1875. The first one-volume edition was published (again by Smith, Elder) in 1877, and *Far from the Madding Crowd* was included in the first collected edition by Osgood, McIlvaine in 1895. The Wessex edition was first published by Macmillan, London, in 1912 and it contains the final revisions made by Hardy to his work. Macmillan's New Wessex edition was published in 1974 and 1975.

Part 2

Summaries
of FAR FROM THE
MADDING CROWD

A general summary

For the purposes of this general summary, the novel is divided into five sections.

1: Oak and Bathsheba (Chapters 1–11)

Gabriel Oak is a young farmer of sound character who is steadily bettering himself by careful management of his sheep. One December he happens to observe the vain self-admiration of a girl – Bathsheba Everdene – who is moving into the neighbourhood. They meet occasionally; he watches her at work and finally proposes marriage, which she refuses. She moves away and takes up the tenancy of her late uncle's farm at Weatherbury. Meanwhile Oak's flock has been accidentally destroyed and he moves away to seek work. He passes a rick fire and, after helping to extinguish it, offers himself as shepherd to the farmer, who turns out to be Bathsheba. She hires him. That evening he passes a timid girl on the road. We later discover that this was Fanny Robin running away to Casterbridge where her lover, Sergeant Troy, is stationed with his regiment; he agrees to marry her. Meanwhile Bathsheba has dismissed her bailiff for stealing and decides to manage the farm herself.

2: Boldwood and Bathsheba (Chapters 12–23)

A neighbour, Farmer Boldwood, calls to enquire after Fanny, but Bathsheba cannot see him. Next market day Bathsheba is the centre of interest at the cornmarket; Boldwood alone pays no attention. Because of this, and in an idle moment, Bathsheba sends him a valentine which stirs and fascinates him. At about this time Troy and Fanny wait by mistake at different churches on their wedding day. Troy is humiliated and angry and will not name another day. Boldwood hesitates to speak to Bathsheba until the end of May, when he makes a proposal of marriage to her, which she refuses. Bathsheba asks Oak for his views which he gives bluntly, and he is consequently dismissed. The next day, however, Bathsheba's sheep fall ill and she begs Oak to return to cure them. After the shearing supper Boldwood proposes again and Bathsheba replies that she hopes to be able to accept him.

3: Troy and Bathsheba (Chapters 24–38)

That night Bathsheba's dress happens to tangle in the rowel of Troy's spur as they pass on the same footpath. She is ruffled but flattered by his impudent admiration of her. He speaks to her again at haymaking and helps her with some bees; finally he demonstrates his dashing military sword-drill to her. Oak tries to warn her about the reputation of Troy, who has now left for Bath, and speaks up for Boldwood. But Bathsheba is desperate to hear only good of Troy and writes to Boldwood saying she cannot marry him. Bathsheba and Boldwood meet by chance, and so fearful is Boldwood's anger that Bathsheba sets out that night for Bath to renounce Troy. They return separately a fortnight later and Boldwood is overcome by rage and grief to discover that they are married. Troy celebrates the harvest supper in August and makes the farmworkers so drunk that they are unable to help Oak to cover the ricks against a dreadful storm that night, although Bathsheba aids him. Boldwood's ricks are neglected.

4: Fanny, Troy and Bathsheba (Chapters 39–48)

In October Bathsheba and Troy pass Fanny on the road. Troy arranges secretly to meet her later in Casterbridge. She struggles to the workhouse but dies in childbirth that night. Bathsheba sends a farmworker to fetch her coffin, but he delays at an inn and the coffin is brought into the house for the night. Bathsheba has her suspicions, although Oak has tried to forestall them, and she finally opens the coffin, discovering Fanny with her child by Troy within. Troy returns and repudiates Bathsheba, declaring that the dead Fanny is morally his wife. Bathsheba rushes out into the dark. Next day Troy remorsefully orders a tomb for Fanny and plants the grave with flowers which are washed away in a downpour. Feeling the pointlessness of this repentant gesture he leaves Weatherbury and, reaching the coast, is swept out to sea while taking a refreshing bathe. He is picked up by a passing boat, although back at home many conclude that he is drowned.

5: Boldwood, Troy, Oak and Bathsheba (Chapters 49–57)

Oak manages both farms as winter and spring pass, and by the summer Boldwood has hopes of being able to speak again of marriage to Bathsheba. Meanwhile Troy is back in Wessex after much travelling and appears in a circus act at the autumn sheep-fair. Bathsheba does not recognise him there and Troy prevents her from being warned of his presence. Boldwood escorts her home that evening and asks her again to marry him when she legally can (Troy's death never having been

proved). She promises an answer at Christmas. Boldwood gives a
Christmas party in Bathsheba's honour and, from a sense of debt and
fear, she agrees to marry him in six years. Troy suddenly appears,
however, to claim Bathsheba, and is shot down by the frenzied
Boldwood who then gives himself up. Bathsheba has the body carried
home where she lovingly prepares it for the grave. The death-sentence
on Boldwood is commuted to life-imprisonment. Bathsheba lives as a
recluse for many months. In August Oak warns her that he will be
leaving in the spring. She receives his resignation after Christmas, and
goes in her desolation to his cottage. There they resolve misunderstand-
ings and agree on a wedding, which is celebrated quietly some time later.

Detailed summaries

Chapter 1: Description of Farmer Oak – An Incident

We are told that Oak is a bachelor of twenty-eight years. He is of sound
judgement and good character, lukewarm of faith, but modest and
unassuming. This December morning he passes a wagon carrying a
handsome girl (we discover in Chapter 4 that this was Bathsheba
Everdene). He watches as she looks at herself in a mirror and notes her
fault of vanity.

NOTES AND GLOSSARY:
Hardy's comment on 'Woman's prescriptive infirmity' is going to be a
vital remark for the study of the whole novel. The reader must ask
whether Bathsheba's vanity is an incurable, and finally uncured, part of
her make-up as a woman.

The reader should also notice Hardy's comment on her apparent
thoughts – 'vistas of probable triumphs'. Bathsheba is to learn that
suffering and disaster can follow from idle victories in romance.

Laodicean: lukewarm of faith (see the Bible, Revelations 3:15, 16)

Communion people: those regularly attending the Christian sacrament of Holy Communion

Nicene creed: statement of Christian belief based on that adopted by first Council of Nicaea, AD325

a coat like Dr Johnson's: in his *Life of Samuel Johnson* (1791) Boswell describes 'a very wide brown cloth great coat, with pockets which might have almost held the two volumes of his folio Dictionary'. Samuel Johnson (1709–84) was a lexicographer, critic and conversationalist; his *Dictionary* was published in 1755

green-faced timekeepers: possibly the greenish brass of the faces of grandfather clocks

fob: a small watch pocket

vestal: a virgin dedicated to Vesta, Roman goddess of the hearth: hence, one who is pure and chaste

prescriptive infirmity: vanity, the weakness ascribed to women

fain would: would have liked to

turnpike gate: a gate set across a road to halt vehicles until the road-toll is paid

higgling: disputable

St John: the Evangelist, who did not desert Christ

Judas Iscariot: the disciple who betrayed Christ (see the Bible, Matthew 26:47) and committed suicide (Matthew 27:5)

Chapter 2: Night – The Flock – An Interior – Another Interior

In contrast to the previous chapter, Hardy describes a desolate midwinter night scene in which man is dwarfed by the vastness of the universe. Oak is tending his sheep and we learn of the precarious state of his affairs, and more of his good sense. The inside of his hut is described. Oak feels himself momentarily separated from the troubles and joys of humanity even as he notices the light from the barn where Bathsheba is working. He watches her through a crack in the roof and finally recognises her as the girl he saw on the wagon.

NOTES AND GLOSSARY:

Milton's *Paradise Lost* provides an interesting motif in the novel. Eve recounts in *Paradise Lost* (IV.1.460) how she looked at herself in a stream – before the Fall – and, like Bathsheba with the mirror, the action is harmless of itself but indicative of inherent vanity. Here Oak looks down on Bathsheba as Satan looked on Paradise. The purpose of the allusion is less to imply any evil intention on Oak's part than to suggest the essential innocence of Bathsheba.

The verbs with which Hardy describes the wind are of unrestrained energy, for instance, 'smote', 'floundered'; and of formless sound, for instance, 'wailed', 'chaunted'. These make a clear contrast with the clarity and sequence of Oak's flute. He is revealed as a man who can create some order out of the arbitrary events of Nature.

St Thomas's: 21 December, the day of St Thomas the Apostle

North Star, Bear, Sirius (the Dog-star), Capella, Aldebaran, Betelgueux, Pleiades, Orion, Castor and Pollux, Square of Pegasus, Vega, Cassiopeia's Chair: all are stars or constellations by which Oak, and all countrymen from the earliest times, can judge the time and seasons

Noah's Ark...Ararat:	the Bible, Genesis 6, recounts how God determines to destroy the world by flood for its evil. Only the good Noah is to be saved (Genesis 6:14) by building an ark (a covered boat). When the floods recede the Ark settles safely on the top of Mount Ararat (Genesis 8:4)
bailiff:	the agent, factor or deputy of a landowner
man:	here, servant
sheep-crook:	shepherd's hooked staff
Milton's Satan:	*Paradise Lost* by John Milton (1608–74) was published in 1667. In Book IV Satan, the defeated rebel angel, looks into Paradise, the blissful abode created by God for man, with the intention of corrupting the innocence of mankind
Devon breed:	a red-coated breed of beef cattle
Lucina:	Roman goddess presiding over childbirth
side-saddle:	saddle for women, designed so that the rider's legs are on the same side of the horse. Riding astride used to be considered improper for a woman
nebula:	a distant cluster of stars

Chapter 3: A Girl on Horseback – Conversation

The next day Oak watches Bathsheba's equestrian antics on her way to the mill. He returns a lost hat to her and embarrasses her by telling her that he had watched her riding. Later that week he nearly suffocates in his hut on a cold night. Bathsheba discovers and rescues him and then teases and flirts with him.

NOTES AND GLOSSARY:
Although we know that Bathsheba cares about the effect she creates, nevertheless this riding scene expresses her independence, freedom from convention and *joie-de-vivre*.

This scene in the hut with Oak may be recalled in Chapter 54 where the dead Troy lies with his head in Bathsheba's lap. Her relationship with these two is often a physical one. With Oak it is of a practical nature: he holds her hands as they grind the shears (Chapter 20), they work side by side in the storm (Chapter 37), and on Fanny's grave (Chapter 46). With Troy the overtones are sexual: the sword-exercise (Chapter 28), his closeness outside the fairground tent (Chapter 50), and her ministrations to his dead body (Chapter 54).

bridle-path:	a path for horses
eight heads:	the artistic proportion of the human frame is held to be eight times the length of the head

Nymphean:	nymphs were semi-divine maidens at large in nature. Hardy is saying that the girl should not be given the fictional beauty of a divinity
conning:	studying her face
acres:	there are almost two and a half acres in a hectare
a stag of ten:	one with ten tines or prongs to his antlers
Maiden's Blush ... Provence ... Crimson Tuscany:	all varieties of rose, each darker than the previous one
yeaning:	lambing
Samson:	In the Bible, Judges 16:20, Samson wakes from his sleep in Delilah's lap and finds that she has shorn him and his strength has left him. He says, 'I will go out as at other times before, and shake myself.' We are invited to consider the parallel of Oak's distraction by a beautiful woman
'ee:	you (thee)

Chapter 4: Gabriel's Resolve – The Visit – The Mistake

Oak watches the girl secretly, feeling more and more attracted to her. He learns her name (and so does the reader) and determines to marry her. He visits her one January morning but is put off by her aunt. Bathsheba runs after him – not to accept him, but also not to lose him.

NOTES AND GLOSSARY:

Their view of marriage sheds light on the course the novel takes. Bathsheba would like the bride's opportunity of showing off, but not her responsibilities. Gabriel's view is nearer that of the 'good fellowship' which they find with each other in the penultimate chapter.

We learn why Oak will not succeed with her now. He is too humble (she needs impressing) and too honest (some deception is required).

'Full of sound ... nothing':	from Macbeth's speech of disillusionment, Shakespeare, *Macbeth*, 5.v
whiting:	chalk prepared as a cleaning material
guano:	the excrement of sea-birds used as a fertiliser
Roman cement:	made by adding water to clay, lime and sand
Commination-service:	part of the service for Ash Wednesday; it contains cursings against sinners and could include their temporary ejection from the church as penance. It is rarely used now
gig:	a light, two-wheeled cart drawn by one horse
Ecclesiastes:	The twenty-first book of the Old Testament. It is not long (twelve chapters) and would well repay reading in the study of this novel. It concerns the

prevalence of vanity and the nature of true wisdom. Two verses are worth quoting here: 'I find more bitter than death the woman, whose heart is snares and nets . . . whoso pleaseth God shall escape from her; but the sinner shall be taken by her' (7:26) and 'In the morning sow thy seed, and in the evening hold not thy hand: for thou knowest not whether shall prosper, either this or that, or whether they both shall be alike good' (11:6). The author uses metaphors of light and darkness and refers particularly to the vulnerability of all men: 'but time and chance happeneth to them all' (9:11)

Chapter 5: Departure of Bathsheba – A Pastoral Tragedy

Bathsheba has gone away to Weatherbury but Oak's love for her grows thereby the deeper. Oak's dogs are described; the good sense of the elder and the foolish assiduousness of the younger. The latter chases the flock over the cliff of a chalk-pit thus leaving Oak virtually penniless.

NOTES AND GLOSSARY:
Hardy makes much use of the effect of light and darkness, the descriptions often reinforcing meaning. The silhouette of the dog is striking as well as the moonlit, deathly pool. Hardy often refers to the colours and techniques of particular paintings in creating effect and makes much use in this novel of the dramatic impact of silhouette. The images of death and decay used here for the pool recur at a turning point in Bathsheba's life (Chapter 44, the hollow in the ferns) and in Fanny's (Chapter 11, outside the barracks).

humours:	disposition, formerly believed to be created by the mixture of the four cardinal body fluids known as the humours
Turner:	J. M. W. Turner (1775–1851), landscape painter, noted for his subtle use of colour
staple:	fibre determining the wool's quality
staggerer:	a staggering blow
down:	undulating upland area
forward ewes:	those lambing early
Hylas . . . Mysian shore:	in Greek mythology Hylas was a beautiful youth beloved by Hercules, whom he accompanied with the Argonauts. When the expedition stopped for water on the coast of Mysia, Hylas was drawn into the fountain by the Naiads and disappeared. Hercules called for him in vain

Napoleon at St Helena: Napoleon Bonaparte (1769–1821), the French Emperor defeated at Waterloo in 1815 and exiled to the island of St Helena, where he died. Hardy is creating bathetic contrast with the lonely figure of the dog which has just destroyed a flock of sheep

Chapter 6: The Fair – The Journey – The Fire

Oak fails to find employment at Casterbridge hiring-fair two months later. He sets out by night for the next fair, near Weatherbury. He comes upon a rick fire which he helps to extinguish. The rick is owned by Bathsheba, who has inherited tenure of the farm from an uncle. Oak offers himself to her as a shepherd.

NOTES AND GLOSSARY:

Oak's setback has served to strengthen some of his characteristics and to give him an elevating indifference to fate.

The final words of the chapter are significant; in the symbolic connotation of 'shepherd' Bathsheba is much in need of someone to aid and guide her.

slime-pits of Siddim: bitumen pits in the area of the Dead Sea. The Bible, Genesis 14:10, recounts how the kings of Sodom and Gomorrah fell into them while fleeing from a battle

smock-frock: a tough linen garment worn as an overall by agricultural workers and decorated with stitched gathers (smocking)

'Jockey to the Fair': an eighteenth-century folksong

Arcadian: in classical tradition the inhabitants of Arcadia were shepherds who worshipped Pan, inventor of the seven-reed pipe. It is thought of as being an ideal pastoral paradise

the god: Morpheus, classical god of dreams and sleep

Charles's Wain and the Pole-star: northern constellation and star

dandy cattle: smart people

lucifer: Smallbury is muddled; 'Lucifer' was the rebel angel who fell through pride, 'a lucifer' was the name for a match

feymell: female

peanner: piano

staddles: stone supports raising the base of a rick above the ground

pitch-and-toss sovereign: a game in which a coin is tossed at a mark. A sovereign was a gold coin worth a pound

Chapter 7: Recognition – A Timid Girl

Oak is taken on as shepherd. Later that night he exchanges a few words with a girl who is leaving Weatherbury (we later learn that this was Fanny Robin).

NOTES AND GLOSSARY:
Oak fancies himself in the shadow of great sadness as he touches Fanny in giving her money. It is true that Fanny's fate is to bring suffering to Troy and Bathsheba also.

Ashtoreth ... Venus: the Roman goddess Venus is familar but her attributes descend from the mysterious cult of Ashtoreth, Zidonian goddess of love. Even the wise Solomon worshipped her, thus angering his own God (see the Bible, I Kings 11:5)

knock in a bit and a drop: eat and drink

Malthouse: a building for preparing and storing barley for brewing and distilling; a warm and congenial place for villagers to meet

femoral artery: large blood-vessel in the upper leg

Chapter 8: The Malthouse – The Chat – News

Hardy introduces, and lightly characterises, the farmworkers. News is brought that Bathsheba has dismissed the bailiff for theft and that Fanny has disappeared, perhaps with a soldier.

NOTES AND GLOSSARY:
Hardy is to keep us reminded of Pennyways, the bailiff, and the grudge he hereafter bears Bathsheba.

louvre-boards: the sides of the little turret are slatted so that air can flow in and out but rain is excluded

Elymas-the-Sorcerer: the Bible, Acts 13:6–12, describes how Paul blinded this false prophet for opposing him and 'he went about seeking some to lead him by the hand' (11). Oak is groping in the dark like a blind man

bobbin: the bar on a string for pulling up the doorlatch

chinchilla: grey; the chinchilla is a South American rodent with grey fur

Purification Day: Candlemas Day, 2 February

use-money: the interest on charitable endowments

gied: given

second-best poor: here, the poorest villagers not actually living in the Union Workhouse

traypse:	traipse – to walk dejectedly
sommit:	something
clane:	clean
chaw:	chew
Saint-Simonian:	the Comte de Saint-Simon (1760–1825) is regarded as the father of French socialism
godfather:	the sponsor at Christian baptism
jerry-go-nimble:	circus
ba'dy:	bawdy
dang:	damn
'a:	he (or she)
Keeper:	gamekeeper, employed to preserve gamebirds and prevent poaching
metheglin:	a kind of spiced mead
the Belief:	the Creed
Dearly Beloved Brethren ... Saying After Me:	the opening and closing words of the exhortation which precedes the Confession at Morning and Evening Prayers
d':	do
o't:	of it
mane:	mean
lime-basket:	lime as a fertiliser would have been spread by hand from a basket
White Monday:	Whit Monday, the day after the Feast of Pentecost (Whitsun)
horned man:	the devil
Nater:	Nature
scores and long-hundreds:	a score is twenty, a long-hundred is one hundred and twenty
the seventh:	the seventh Commandment: see the Bible, Exodus 20:14, 'Thou shalt not commit adultery'
confirmed:	he underwent the rite administered to baptised Christians confirming their faith
clerk:	a lay officer of a parish church; he would assist with the responses during services
Let Your Light so Shine:	from the Bible, Matthew 5:16; the words are spoken before the Offertory at the Anglican Communion Service
charity-boys:	those brought up in charitable institutions
chiel:	child
baily:	bailiff
the Devil's head in a cowl:	that is, Pennyways' real nature is disguised
three-double:	folded in three
yer:	your

as lief as not:	be happy to
'Dame Durden':	a folksong about a woman who kept five serving-maids and five serving-men
Minerva:	the Roman goddess of war, but also of wisdom and the arts. She invented the flute but was disgusted with the way playing it distorted her features
as if hung in wires:	like a puppet
fleed at:	flew at
persecute:	prosecute
neck and crop	headlong
news-bell:	a ringing sound in the ears was supposed to foretell bad news
magpie all alone:	seeing a single magpie means bad luck; the rhyme goes up to seven and begins, 'One for sorrow, two for joy . . .'
crowner's inquest:	a coroner's enquiry into the cause of a death
Gabriel's books:	*The Pilgrim's Progress* (1678) by John Bunyan, (1628–88), an allegorical tale of a man's moral progress; *Robinson Crusoe* (1719) by Daniel Defoe, (?1660–1731), an adventure story describing how the hero skilfully survived the wreck of his ship. The titles of the rest are self-explanatory. These books show Oak's interest in practical matters which concern his livelihood as well as in philosophical, moral and religious questions. In addition to practical manuals, he also possesses books with which to improve his own education and general knowledge
furlong:	one-eighth of a mile, or 201 metres

Chapter 9: The Homestead – A Visitor – Half-Confidences

Bathsheba's home and servant-girls are described. Her neighbour, Farmer Boldwood, calls to enquire after Fanny but Bathsheba will not see him because she is untidy from her housework.

NOTES AND GLOSSARY:
Bathsheba's first information about Boldwood concerns his indifference to women. From her annoyance at her disarray it is clear that she is annoyed at not having met him.

Classic Renaissance: the period of English architecture beginning in the mid-sixteenth century. Hardy describes the house with the accuracy of his architectural training; it is a mixture of the Classical with the earlier Gothic style

manorial hall:	the house reserved as the home of the Lord of the Manor. Some editions have 'memorial' (that is, the office containing the steward's estate records)
demesnes:	estates
fluted pilasters:	decorative columns set in the wall and having vertical grooves cut in them
coped gables:	the upper, triangular part of a house's end wall is the gable. Sometimes this is raised above the level of the roof by coping stones as both ornament and weather-proofing
finials:	ornaments on the apex of a gable
Gothic:	the pointed-arch architecture prevalent from the twelfth to the sixteenth century
houseleek:	or sengreen, a plant of the stonecrop family, often growing on roofs
balusters:	posts supporting the handrails of the staircase
Terberg:	Gerard Terberg or Terborch (1617–81), a Dutch portrait and genre painter
Gerard Douw:	(also Dow or Dou, 1613–75) Dutch painter who studied under Rembrandt
Normandy pippin:	apple with a yellowish shrivelled skin
thirtover:	thwartover, that is, perverse
Not-at-homes:	a euphemism for being unwilling to see a caller
fright:	looking untidy
scanning measure:	accenting both syllables of 'penny' as in the metrical unit known as a spondee
staid:	steady and sober
pucker:	state of excitement and fuss
a pelican in the wilderness:	from the Bible, Psalm 102:6; alone
Chain Salpae:	a salp is a small, proto-chordate marine animal. Its stolon divides into chains of segments, each of which eventually forms a new individual
Russia duck:	strong, plain woven material, originating in Russia and used for making outer garments
drabbet:	unbleached linen of a drab colour used for making smock-frocks
honeycomb work:	the material is gathered in crossing lines which gives the effect of a honeycomb
pattens:	overshoes with a raised sole for keeping the wearer's shoes above the mud
Philistines:	the Philistines harassed the Israelites. The word is now used for those thought to be uncultured and concerned with base and material interests. The reference is to the Bible, Judges 16:9

Chapter 10: Mistress and Men

Bathsheba gets to know her men as she pays their wages. News is brought that Fanny has followed the regiment of Dragoon Guards away from Casterbridge.

NOTES AND GLOSSARY:
We learn more of Bathsheba's farmworkers here; they are the chief means by which Hardy introduces humour into the novel, although they do have an important role as commentators (or chorus) on the main events.

time-book:	a book for recording the workmen's hours of work, on which their wages were calculated
cuss	curse
Temperance and Soberness:	naming children after abstract qualities was part of the Puritan tradition
thrashing-machine:	device for beating grain from the head of corn
wimbling haybonds:	making hayropes with a tool called a wimble
Early Flourballs ... Thompson's Wonderfuls:	varieties of potato
dibble:	a tool for making holes in the ground
scarlet:	here, willing to have sexual intercourse
gawkhammer:	awkward and stupid
hustings:	the platform from which Parliamentary candidates were nominated
Cain and Abel:	sons of Adam and Eve. Genesis 4 recounts how Cain killed Abel because his brother's sacrifice was better received by God
en:	him
in the writings of the later poets ... reserve:	the ancient Greek poet Homer places the kingdom of the Gods on Mount Olympus. They do become loftier, in both senses, in the poetry of the 'later' Roman poets who place their kingdom in the sky. Jove was the Roman equivalent of the Greek Zeus and was chief of all the Gods
in round numbers:	putting it simply
Dragoon Guards:	cavalry regiment armed with carbines (which breathed fire like dragons)
Route:	marching orders
like a thief in the night:	from the Bible, I Thessalonians 5:2; 'the day of the Lord so cometh as a thief in the night'
nameless women:	prostitutes
thesmothete:	lawgiver (the ancient Greek title for the six junior chief magistrates in Athens)

Chapter 11: Outside the Barracks – Snow – A Meeting

After a snowstorm Fanny speaks to Troy through a window in the barracks. He agrees to marry her.

NOTES AND GLOSSARY:
Troy's attitude to Fanny is clearly irresponsible and callous, but not absolutely unkind.

banns: notice declared three times in church of intended marriage
licence: permit to marry granted, in lieu of banns, by the bishop
published: the banns would have to be read in the parish church in which each resided

Chapter 12: Farmers – A Rule – An Exception

Bathsheba carries on the farm business herself, negotiating prices at Casterbridge cornmarket on the next market-day. As a woman, if not as a farmer, she is the object of interest and admiration by all – except for one man, whom Hardy describes. Bathsheba discovers that this man is Boldwood.

NOTES AND GLOSSARY:
by proxy: using an agent
cornmarket: large building used for the exchange and trade of grain
chaise: a light, open travelling carriage drawn by ponies

Chapter 13: Sortes Sanctorum – The Valentine

It is 13 February and Bathsheba, as a game, uses the Bible and a key for the old superstitious practice of foretelling her husband. From some pique at being ignored by Boldwood, but leaving the final decision to the chance fall of a tossed book, she sends him a valentine.

NOTES AND GLOSSARY:
The words of the minor characters are often more significant than anyone realises. Here the maid Liddy comments of Boldwood, 'He'd worry to death' over the valentine.

Bathsheba is prompted by Liddy ('like a little brook . . . shallow') and Hardy is at pains to stress the idle and off-hand spirit in which the card is sent. We are warned of Bathsheba's ignorance of the subjective power of love (and thereby her blindness to the possible consequences of this deed) although this is not necessarily going to exonerate her.

Sortes Sanctorum: 'oracles of the Holy Scriptures'; this was a method of fortune-telling by which the Bible was opened at random and the first words to be read provided the prophecy. What Bathsheba actually did with the Bible and key is not absolutely clear; R. L. Purdy's Riverside edition (Boston, 1957) describes an illustration in which the book has been closed over the key and Bathsheba and Liddy wait to see if the key will move as she repeats the verse from Ruth – the Book which tells how Ruth won Boaz for her husband

thirteenth of February: the eve of St Valentine's day when cards of the sort described here are sent, often in jest, to a member of the opposite sex

quarto Bible: Bible printed on small, quarto-sized sheets of paper

the sublime words: held to be Ruth 1:16

post-octavo: an even smaller size of paper than quarto

Daniel . . . kneeling eastward: Daniel was a Jewish captive in Babylon (see the Bible, Daniel 1). He was cast into a den of lions for persisting in praying in defiance of King Darius (Daniel 6:10, 16)

Chapter 14: Effect of the Letter – Sunrise

Boldwood is fascinated next day by the anonymous card, ascribing a deliberate motive to its sender. By chance he opens a letter of Oak's and in going to return it is provided with an opportunity of speaking to the shepherd.

NOTES AND GLOSSARY:
Hardy clearly draws a distinction here between those who allow circumstances to follow each other in a natural chain of events (Hardy repeatedly uses the word 'groove') and those who superimpose their own will on what happens. This theme runs throughout the novel and it necessarily includes consideration of the influence of chance and coincidence.

Columbus: Christopher Columbus made his first voyage to the New World in 1492, when the presence of land was indicated by floating seaweed

yeoman: freehold farmer of the middle class

zenith: the point of the sky directly above the observer

ewe-lease: sheep pasture

Venetian glass: Venice is still famous for the artistry of its ornamental glassware

Chapter 15: A Morning Meeting – The Letter again

That same morning the farmworkers are discussing Bathsheba's farm management and, until Oak stops such talk, they prophesy ruin from her pride and vanity. Boldwood appears with Oak's letter. It is from Fanny, returning his money and announcing that she is to be married to Troy. Oak identifies Bathsheba's writing on the valentine for Boldwood.

NOTES AND GLOSSARY:

Fanny's letter provides an introduction to Troy's character. She writes of 'a man of great respectability and high honour', but the reader must beware of her judgement for several reasons: she is an unsophisticated country girl who loves him and so may be blind to his faults; he may have deceived her (Boldwood thinks he has); and she may be over-impressed by his noble blood and military rank, which she states very proudly.

a hyperbolic curve: the point about a hyperbolic curve is that the longer it is the nearer it approaches its axes, but it will only meet them at infinity

pipkin: a small earthenware pot

snapper: frost (a cold snap)

kerseymere: twilled fine woollen cloth

Joey Iscariot: see Chapter 1

travel: trouble

martel: mortal

entr'acte: a separate performance between two acts of a play

dulcimer: a musical instrument with strings over a sounding board, not unlike a piano

tined: closed

Lady Day: 25 March, the Feast of the Annunciation and a quarter-day for payment of rent, making of agreements, and so on. (This is late for lambing to finish in the South of England)

Sexajessamine Sunday: Poorgrass's pronounciation of Sexagesima; the second Sunday before Lent (this would be early for lambing to finish)

rooted: uprooted

hogshead: a large cask for holding $52\frac{1}{2}$ imperial gallons (about 240 litres)

smack-and-coddle: kiss and cuddle

Thor: Scandinavian god of thunder who possessed a magical stone hammer

sun-dials: a clock which tells the time by a shadow cast on its face by the sun

prent: print

copper-plate: a particularly neat style of handwriting

a nobleman by blood: Troy is the bastard son of the Earl of Severn (Chapter 26)

fold: an enclosure for sheep

Chapter 16: All Saints' and All Souls'

On their wedding day Troy waits at one church and Fanny, by mistake, at another. When they meet he feels too humiliated and angry to arrange another time and simply leaves her.

NOTES AND GLOSSARY:
Here chance dictates that the couple should mistake churches but Troy, with his injured pride, does not actively reverse the chance mistake but passively allows events to take their course (see notes above on Chapter 14). Hardy wrote this chapter as an afterthought, when he had finished the rest of the novel.

quarter-jack: a mechanical figure (automaton, or mannikin) which strikes the clock bell at every quarter-hour

almsmen: men supported by charity

Chapter 17: In the Market-place

The following Saturday, at the cornmarket, Boldwood cannot take his eyes or his thoughts from Bathsheba. She realises this but does not value the attention, having won it by ingenuity. She is sorry for having teased a man she respects.

NOTES AND GLOSSARY:

Adam ... Eve: the first man and woman created by God (Genesis 1 and 2); they are corrupted by Satan in the form of a serpent

R.A.'s: Royal Academician's; one who, being an artist, should be an authority on beauty

'the injured lover's hell': from *Paradise Lost* V, 449, where Milton speaks of Eve's beauty and the freedom of the Sons of God from the hell of jealousy in contemplating her

Chapter 18: Boldwood in Meditation – Regret

Boldwood's character is further described: he is a man of deep feeling; any emotion which possesses him at all possesses him entirely; he is pre-eminently serious. He is too shy to speak to Bathsheba as she works with Oak and her lambs.

NOTES AND GLOSSARY:
Hardy tells us clearly here that Bathsheba is not a schemer and trifler like a real flirt, although this is how she may seem.

a Moorish arch: rounded – more like a horseshoe than the back of the horse itself

almonry and cloister: Hardy goes on to expand this image: after overseeing the feeding of his horses (like almsgiving) Boldwood walks and meditates here (like a monk in a cloister)

acquainted with grief: (see the Bible, Isaiah 53:3)

Dryads: wood-nymphs; semi-divine maidens living in trees

the uncertain glory of an April day: from Shakespeare, *Two Gentlemen of Verona*, 1, iii. April in England can be a mixture of bright sun and showers

cabala: secret

Chapter 19: The Sheep-washing – The Offer

While her men are dipping the sheep at the end of May Boldwood makes an offer of marriage to Bathsheba which she refuses. She regrets the suffering she has caused him.

NOTES AND GLOSSARY:
Like Oak's (see Chapter 4), Boldwood's first observation of Bathsheba is from a distance. But where Oak envisaged the practicalities of marriage to her (a ten-pound gig for market, cocks and hens, a cucumber frame) Boldwood is idealising her.

Cyclops' eye: in Classical mythology the Cyclops were a gigantic race of lawless shepherds, each having only one eye in the middle of his forehead

Chapter 20: Perplexity – Grinding the Shears – A Quarrel

Bathsheba's reason tells her that Boldwood would be the right husband, and her honesty that she ought to repair the damage she has caused. But she is not ready for marriage and enjoys control of the farm. Grinding the sheep-shears with Oak the next day she asks his opinion. His reply is to reprimand her and, piqued, she orders him off the farm.

NOTES AND GLOSSARY:

Elizabeth: (1533–1603) Queen of England and Ireland. She was a clever, intelligent and well-educated woman who was able to survive politically in a difficult and dangerous man's world

Mary:	(1542–87) Queen of Scots. She was educated in France and regarded as frivolous on her return to Scotland in 1561. She was a controversial woman, indulging in erratic political intrigue and injudicious love-affairs
scurr:	the sound of a tool being sharpened
Eros:	the boy-god of love who shoots his arrows blindly
Ixion:	in Greek mythology he was the King of Thessaly who was tied for eternity to a wheel of fire for trying to seduce Zeus's wife. Turning a wheel can daze the mind, and Hardy refers to the depressing use of the treadmill in nineteenth-century gaols
a Danby sunset:	either Francis Danby (1793–1861) or his son James (1816–75), landscape painters noted for the brilliancy of their dawn and sunset scenes
Moses . . . Pharaoh:	in the Bible, Exodus recounts how Moses sought the release from captivity by Pharaoh of the Israelites. In Exodus 10:28, 29 Pharaoh orders him to leave ('see my face no more') and Moses's reply is measured and dignified

Chapter 21: Troubles in the Fold – A Message

A day later, fifty-seven of Bathsheba's sheep stray into a field of clover and become bloated. Only Oak knows how to cure them and he returns to help after insisting that Bathsheba ask him politely. He is reinstated on the farm.

NOTES AND GLOSSARY:
Here, as with the fire (Chapter 6) and the storm (Chapter 37) Oak is able, by his skill, patience and presence of mind, to make the best of a natural disaster; and on these occasions it is to Bathsheba's benefit.

blasted:	bloated; the abdomen of the beast is distended by gas from its gorging on over-rich pasture
Ephesians:	the Epistle of Paul to the Ephesians is quite short and might well be overlooked between the longer I and II Corinthians and I and II Thesalonians. Ephesians contains the famous description of the strength of the man who puts on 'the whole armour of God'
'Swoln with wind and the rank mist they drew':	from Milton's poem 'Lycidas' 1.126. The passage is ostensibly describing neglected sheep but it is an implicit attack on the failings of the Church

store ewes:	ewes retained on the farm either for fattening or for breeding
holler:	hollow
Morton's . . . Shrewsbury:	In Shakespeare's *2 Henry IV*, 1. i, Morton, a retainer of the Earl of Northumberland, arrives in distress to announce the death of the Earl's son Hotspur at the battle of Shrewsbury
lettre-de-cachet:	a summons requiring instant obedience
'ooman:	woman
trochar:	or trocar; a sharp lance inside a hollow tube. The lance was used to pierce the sheep's bloated stomach and the gas escaped through the tube when the lance was withdrawn
rumen:	the first stomach of a cud-chewing animal

Chapter 22: The Great Barn and the Sheep-shearers

It is 1 June and Bathsheba's sheep are being shorn in the great barn, whose antiquity and pristine condition speak of the timelessness of the occupations it is used for. While Oak is enjoying Bathsheba's presence there, Boldwood appears and takes her away to see his sheep. Speculation among the shearers concludes that Bathsheba and Boldwood will soon be married.

NOTES AND GLOSSARY:

A particular concern of Hardy's, more apparent in later novels, is the destruction of the countryside and its occupations, traditions and values by industrialisation and mechanisation. There is some evidence of this feeling in his frequent reference in this novel to townsfolk as somehow different from and inferior to country people.

spring tides . . . neap:	the high tide mark is at its highest at the spring tides and its lowest at neap tides
bishops' crozier:	an ornamented hooked staff, symbolic of the bishop's role of shepherd or spiritual guardian of the Christians in his diocese or area
malachite:	green mineral which will take a high polish
catkins, fern-sprouts, moschatel, ladies' smocks, toothwort, enchanter's nightshade, doleful-bells:	these plants do not really need explaining individually; they are all unusual in some way – in appearance, scent or habitat
high and low caste Hindoo:	caste is the rigid social division among those of the Hindu faith
transepts:	the north and south sections of any church which is shaped like a cross

chestnut:	the roof-frame would have been made of durable Spanish chestnut wood
collars:	horizontal beams connecting two rafters thus making an A-shaped roof-truss
curves and diagonals:	timbers positioned for further support of the roof
striding buttresses:	or flying buttresses; supports built outside the wall to carry the weight-thrust of the roof
lancet:	a narrow, pointed window
abraded:	worn by use and weathered by time
lanceolate:	shaped like a spear-head
chamfers:	the bevelled edges of the stonework
axis:	the focal point of the building's proportions
flail:	a hand tool for threshing grain
Elizabethan:	of the reign of Elizabeth I (see Chapter 20)
nave:	west end of a church
chancel:	east end of a church, sometimes railed off; reserved for choir and clergy
wimble:	a tool for twisting loose material into ropes (see Chapter 10)
Guildenstern:	one of the courtiers in Shakespeare's *Hamlet*; Hamlet asks how he is and Guildenstern replies, 'Happy in that we are not overhappy'; contented with a middle state which may be maintained
Aphrodite:	Greek goddess of beauty and love. Said to have risen from the foam arising when the severed genitals of Uranus fell into the sea
shearling:	a sheep that has been shorn once
hog:	a young sheep before its first shearing
spreading-board:	board on which a sheep is laid to be shorn
St John Long:	(1798–1834) an Irish quack doctor who, when ill, would not submit to his own painful treatment for consumption (tuberculosis)
better wed over the mixen than over the moor:	an old saying; it is better to marry a neighbour than someone from distant parts (mixen is a dungheap)
scarn:	scorn
spear-bed:	reed bed
pharisaical:	superior (but with a hint of hypocrisy, since Oak does not know all that passed)
gird at:	mock
linsey:	a coarse cloth made from a mixture of linen and wool
Nicholas Poussin:	French historical and landscape painter (1594–1665) notable as a master of the Classical form

'I find more bitter . . . snares and nets': (see the note to Chapter 4). There, because the skittishness of Bathsheba is so trivial in comparison with the solemnity of Ecclesiastes, Oak is really presented as over-reacting and therefore somewhat comic. Here, however, he is beginning to understand the real trouble that Bathsheba can cause; although he 'adored [her] just the same'

junketing: feasting
puddens: puddings
horse-bean: a coarse bean used for fodder
brandise: grate
biffens: deep red cooking apples

Chapter 23: Eventide – A Second Declaration

After the shearing supper that evening Boldwood has made a second declaration of love to Bathsheba. She replies that she hopes to be able to promise to marry him within a few weeks, when he will have returned from an absence.

NOTES AND GLOSSARY:
Hardy is still keeping Bathsheba's vanity before us. Here, although she is pained by Boldwood's distress and is prepared to pay an uncongenial penalty for having caused it, she is nevertheless flattered by his idolising of her and pleased with her triumph ('the situation was not without a fearful joy').

ballet: ballad
composure: composing
'I sowed the seeds . . .': an English folksong – not composed by Poorgrass
Silenus . . . Chromis and Mnasylus: in Virgil's Eclogue 6, two shepherd boys force the drunken Silenus to sing. He goes on and on until night falls. Publius Vergilius Maro (70–19BC) was a Roman poet who wrote epic and didactic poetry as well as the pastoral verse of the *Eclogues*
'The Banks of Allan Water': a traditional air, the words being by M. G. Lewis (1775–1818)
attar: essence
Keats . . . a too happy happiness: reference to the ode 'To a Nightingale' by John Keats (1795–1821). Keats describes himself as somehow removed from reality by the beauty of the song ('a drowsy numbness pains/My sense'); so is Boldwood transformed by his love

Chapter 24: The same Night – The Fir Plantation

After making her evening round of the farm that night and while passing through a plantation, Bathsheba finds her dress has become entangled in the spur of Troy, who is also on the footpath. He praises her beauty and she returns home flattered and fascinated.

NOTES AND GLOSSARY:
Troy's first meeting with Bathsheba does not have the critical, moral overtone of Oak's (he observes her vanity in Chapter 1) nor is it like the public meeting with, and private apotheosis by, Boldwood in the cornmarket. This is the stark but mutually attractive confrontation of the sexes ('Are you a woman? . . . I am a man') and it takes little account of moral judgements or romantic ideals.

Bathsheba's vanity is still dictating her actions. She does not rip the dress away because it is the one which suits her best, and she ends by thinking well of the impudence which had praised her. The reader is surely invited to recall the unfallen Eve.

stentorian:	very loud. Stentor was the Greek herald in the Trojan war. His voice was as loud as that of fifty men
the ninth plague of Egypt:	through Moses God sent plagues upon Egypt as a means of persuading Pharaoh to let the Israelites depart (see the Bible, Exodus 10:22, which describes 'a thick darkness in all the land of Egypt')
genius loci:	(*Latin*) the presiding spirit of a place
gimp:	a wired silk or cotton cord for trimming a dress
rowel:	the spiked wheel on the end of a horseman's spur
liliputian:	very tiny. Jonathan Swift's hero Gulliver visits Liliput, the land of minute people, in the first book of *Gulliver's Travels* (1726). Swift (1667–1745) is best known for his satiric writing
knots of knots:	marriage
furlough:	a soldier's leave of absence
dand:	dandy
doctor's son by name . . . an earl's son by nature:	compare Fanny's letter, Chapter 15
Grammar School:	these were originally schools founded in the sixteenth century for the teaching of Latin

Chapter 25: The New Acquaintance described

Hardy describes Troy as a man of the present. In that he never looks forward, many of man's finer feelings are unknown to him, and thus material matters seem more important than the possession of moral or aesthetic discrimination. Troy has never been bothered by lack of these feelings and, fully enjoying the present moment, he might superficially appear to have a greater capacity for them. He is untruthful to women, but not absolutely wicked; he acts by impulses, not directing them but allowing his valuable attributes to be wasted in chance and 'useless grooves'. He can be one thing and seem another. It is unlikely that flattery will conquer a woman, Hardy says, although many understand that they may thereby gain power. Troy is one who experiments with flattery, rather than reason, with women. A week or two after the shearing he joins Bathsheba at the haymaking.

NOTES AND GLOSSARY:

Troy's unscrupulousness in lying, and his power of seeming, both remind us of the Satan of *Paradise Lost*, as well as Hardy's comment on the truth taught to many that a flatterer may 'acquire powers reaching to the extremity of perdition.'

lied like a Cretan:	long after the decline of their own great civilisation, the Cretans became a byword for degenerate morals and character
regrater:	a retailer
Corinthian:	a man given to fashionable dissipation
passados:	thrusts in fencing
nankeen:	a yellowish cotton cloth
windrows:	hay is raked into rows when cut, in order to be dried by the wind

Chapter 26: Scene on the Verge of the Hay-mead

By his quick repartee and constant repetition of the words 'beautiful', 'pretty', and 'loveliness' to Bathsheba, Troy gets her to admit, implicitly, that she is proud of her looks. His flattery takes the form of mock admonition and she enjoys the role of one being checked. (It is surely not by coincidence that the early death of her father is mentioned here.) She does perceive his cajolery, calls him flatterer and dissembler, and accuses him of pretending. He spontaneously gives her his gold watch, telling her that he loves her and suddenly seeing her, with some genuineness, as being as beautiful as he had called her. Bathsheba returns the watch but is left bemused and uncertain.

NOTES AND GLOSSARY:

Again Hardy alludes to the temptation of Eve in Paradise: the pastoral setting is idyllic but 'the devil smiled from a loop-hole in Tophet' as she admits to knowledge of her beauty. Troy is constantly referred to as an actor and dissembler.

penchant:	inclination
the third of that Terrible Ten ... the ninth:	the third of the Ten Commandments forbids blasphemy, and the ninth bearing false witness (lying)
Tophet:	Tophet was in the Valley of Hinnom near Jerusalem. Child sacrifice to Moloch was made there and later it became a refuse-dump. It has become synonymous with hell – a place of fiery torment
John Knox:	a Scottish divine (1505–72) who laboured for the reform of the church; he was a disciple of Calvin and his antagonism to the Roman Catholic church led him into conflict with his Catholic Queen, Mary (see Chapter 20)
ewe-lamb:	one's most cherished possession (the Bible, II Samuel 11, 12 recounts how King David took Uriah's wife Bathsheba – his ewe-lamb, 12:3 – and had Uriah killed)
cedit amor rebus:	*(Latin)* from Ovid, *Remedia Amoris*, I, 144. Publius Ovidius Naso (43BC–18AD) was a Roman narrative and elegiac poet

---

Chapter 27: Hiving the Bees

The next day Troy hives a difficult swarm of bees for Bathsheba. He happens to mention his military sword-drill and she expresses a wish to see it. They arrange a meeting for the purpose.

NOTES AND GLOSSARY:
Hardy draws our attention to the operation of chance in Bathsheba's relationship with Troy. It so happens that the bees are unruly, making Bathsheba's job difficult; 'whimsical fate' ordains that she should have the physical contact of dressing him in her hat and gloves; she has heard of the sword-drill from those who 'by chance' have seen it.

espalier:	a tree trained against a fence
costard:	a type of apple tree
quarrenden:	(or quarenden); another type of apple tree, from Devon or Somerset

---

Chapter 28: The Hollow amid the Ferns

Troy and Bathsheba meet in a ferny hollow that evening and he dazzles and bemuses her with the dexterity of his sword-drill, finally leaving her with a kiss which stirs her physically and emotionally.

NOTES AND GLOSSARY:

Here Bathsheba dominates no longer. Hitherto Troy has played the role of servant to her: making her hay, hiving her bees. Now he dictates the action and she is afraid, amazed, astonished – 'overcome by a hundred tumultuous feelings'.

We later learn (Chapter 41) that Troy has a lock of Fanny's hair in his possession. With this gesture of Troy's Hardy recalls Alexander Pope's (1688–1744) mock-heroic poem 'The Rape of the Lock' (1712) in which Pope tries to calm the hot passions raised by the theft of a lady's curl. With the allusion he recalls, too, the pride, vanity, selfishness and false values of those involved in Pope's episode.

brake:	woodland; brake fern is bracken
cut:	a cut is made with the front edge or the first third of the back of the sword
guard:	the position of defence
broadsword:	following the development of the narrow rapier, in the early eighteenth century a stouter, broader, single-edged sword was adopted for military use
aurora militaris:	(*Latin*) dazzling swordplay is a rough translation although Hardy is trying to evoke the effect of the Northern Lights (*aurora borealis*)
scarf-skin:	the outermost layer of skin
Moses in Horeb:	Moses strikes a rock and there pours out a God-given stream of water for the Israelites (see the Bible, Exodus 17:6)

Chapter 29: Particulars of a Twilight Walk

Hardy tells us that her love for Troy has introduced folly into Bathsheba's character. She does not use her discretion in judging if he is deceitful but follows the pleasanter guide of impulse. The judgement is made harder by Troy's surface attractiveness, his faults being hidden deep. Oak is worried for her, and one evening as she walks alone he determines to speak. She rejects his plea for Boldwood and condemnation of Troy and leaves him, then meeting Troy by chance. Oak finds proof that Troy has been lying to her.

NOTES AND GLOSSARY:

Although in Chapter 20 we have been told that Bathsheba is a woman who 'frequently appealed to her understanding' here, as in the sending of the valentine, we are told that she does not control impulse by appeal to her reason in assessing consequences. Hardy ascribes this deficiency to the fact of her womanhood, 'she had too much womanliness to use her understanding to the best advantage'.

From the beginning Oak has rarely talked to Bathsheba with tact nor, from honesty, made any more concessions to her vanity than Boldwood has, from ignorance. He makes no headway in argument here, although Bathsheba is conscious of her weak position, and he does not present her with his concrete evidence (the unused church door) of Troy's deceit.

lymph:	the word has a number of connotations. Physiologically, lymph is a colourless body fluid and there is, perhaps, a suggestion that folly has been introduced into her character just as vaccine-lymph is introduced into the body. In the seventeenth century the word lymphatic bore the connotation of 'frenzied'
tything:	the Saxon division of communities into ten households, each responsible for the peaceable behaviour of the rest
'reck'd not her own rede':	did not take her own advice. The line is from Shakespeare's *Hamlet*, 1. iii, where Ophelia urges her brother Laertes to follow his own good counsels to her
Hippocrates:	(*c.*460–377BC), a Greek physician, known as the 'Father of Medicine'. This 'observation' is from his *Aphorisms* (II, 46): 'When two pains occur together, but not in the same place, the more violent obscures the other'
palter:	equivocate
pretend:	aspire

Chapter 30: Hot Cheeks and Tearful Eyes

Troy leaves for Bath and, half an hour after this meeting, Bathsheba writes to Boldwood telling him she cannot marry him. Then she bursts in on her maids who are talking about her and Troy. She is in an emotional tumult, first denying that she cares for him, then admitting to Liddy that she loves him to distraction. She is desperate to hear good of him but appears afraid that the bad things Oak has spoken of him may be true.

NOTES AND GLOSSARY:

We are told that Bathsheba fears a meeting between Oak and Troy – as between Boldwood and Troy in the next chapter. She knows the force of her influence on them, and is beginning to consider consequences. Again, the conflict between her good sense and her womanliness is stressed as she bursts into the kitchen after hearing herself mentioned. The idea of the unreasoning nature of women is not peculiar to Hardy and recurs in English literature from the Middle Ages.

| Union: | the Union Workhouse was erected by several parishes of a particular district for their paupers. Bathsheba is distraught and confused, but this self-dramatisation is nevertheless unpleasing when one thinks of Fanny who *is* friendless and who *does* die in the Union |
| Amazonian: | the Amazons were a race of warlike women fabled to have lived in Scythia. In fact, we have seen Bathsheba both acting like a tomboy (Chapter 3) and doing a man's job; but she still wishes to have the attractiveness and attention of a woman |

Chapter 31: Blame – Fury

The next morning, by chance, Bathsheba meets the returning Boldwood as she walks out on a visit. He repeats his love for her, attracted first by the valentine. She is repentant, pities him, but is unmoved from the decision expressed in her letter. She admits that Troy has her affection and Boldwood, made furious by his loss both of dignity and of Bathsheba, threatens to punish Troy. Knowing that Troy is about to return, and that a meeting might result in aggression by one and revenge by the other, Bathsheba is at a loss what to do.

NOTES AND GLOSSARY:
We are told that Bathsheba is unable to direct her will into any groove for resolving the difficult situation with Boldwood. It is he who energetically directs their conversation, she whose answers are timid, questioning or petulant.

hurdler and cattle-crib-maker:	a man who makes temporary fences (hurdles) and mangers for cattle fodder (cribs)
tergiversation:	changing her mind
punctilios:	small points of courtesy
amaranthine:	purple colour

Chapter 32: Night – Horses tramping

Seeing someone lead away one of Bathsheba's horses in the dark that night, the charwoman wakes Coggan (a farmworker) and Oak who pursue the thief on two of Boldwood's horses. They find it is Bathsheba herself and she coolly sends them home. We learn that Bathsheba is going to meet Troy, albeit with the intention of renouncing him.

NOTES AND GLOSSARY:
Bathsheba has decided that she cannot leave things to take their course

but must initiate some action. Hardy leaves us to decide whether this decision to see Troy again is simply misguided or self-deceiving.

pinchbeck repeater: pinchbeck is a gold-like alloy of copper and zinc used for making cheap jewellery (named after its inventor). A repeater is a watch which strikes the hours

turnpike-road: a main highway maintained by the tolls collected at turnpikes (see Chapter 1)

byway: a secluded road or track

Chapter 33: In the Sun – A Harbinger

Bathsheba has been away for a fortnight. The farmworkers are harvesting oats when Oak's young assistant, Cain Ball, arrives, having been to Bath. He has seen Bathsheba and Troy there, arm-in-arm like a very familiar courting couple. Oak is agitated by this news, but holds his peace.

NOTES AND GLOSSARY:

Gilpin's rig: John Gilpin was the hero of a comic ballad by William Cowper (1731–1800); it describes his adventures on a runaway horse and the 'rig' (frolic) he had with it

Lammas: 1 August; here, the season around this festival

felon: like a whitlow, an abscess around the finger-nail

All-Fours: a card game

bushel ... Sermon on the Mount ... meek: 'bushel' was a measure of 8 gallons (approximately 36 litres). The reference is to Christ's Sermon from a hilltop (see the Bible, Matthew 5:15) where good men are urged to set an example, ('Neither do men light a candle, and put it under a bushel') and in which the meek are counted among the blessed, 'for they shall inherit the earth' (5). For all his diffidence Poorgrass has an inflated idea of his own worthiness

Tom Putt and a Rathe-ripe: varieties of red and yellow apple

stun-poll: stupid blockhead

kingdom of Bath: Bath is not a kingdom, of course; but to Poorgrass it is far away and very grand

hae: have

hobbed: hobnailed; these were nails with large heads which kept the soles of working boots off the ground

batty-cake: batter-cakes; probably like small pancakes

baking trendle: a large circular tray used by bakers

club-walking:	gathering of members of the parish club, a society whose purpose was partly welfare and partly social
White Tuesday:	the Tuesday of Whit week (see also Chapter 8)
Moses:	Aaron was his brother. (See also Chapters 20 and 28)
fokes:	folk

High Church and High Chapel: the implication of Cain's comment is that the nonconformist chapels are as concerned with the forms of worship as the Anglican churches – but with stress on sparseness rather than elaborateness

she'll wish her cake dough: she'll wish she was back where she started

babe and suckling: a reference to the Bible, Psalm 8:2; Poorgrass loves to lend importance to his remarks by clothing them in biblical language (compare Chapter 57, 'my scripture manner')

blood-stone: Poorgrass, as usual, is sounding very impressive but is totally muddled. By 'blood-stone' he may mean 'birth-stone'; or the precious stone assigned to the time of one's birth. St Matthew was not a prophet but one of Christ's disciples, and in his Gospel he recounts how Jesus quoted Psalm 118:22 concerning the stone which the builders rejected; Jesus adds, 'but on whomsoever it shall fall, it will grind him to powder'. (Matthew 21:44)

Shimei, the son of Gera a supporter of Saul, Shimei cursed King David who was fleeing from Saul's son (see the Bible, II Samuel 16:5–14)

Chapter 34: Home again – A Trickster

Bathsheba comes home again that evening. Boldwood, unaware of her visit to Bath, calls to apologise for his behaviour at their previous meeting, but Bathsheba will not see him. Boldwood sees Troy returning to Weatherbury and accosts him, offering him money to marry Fanny and leave Bathsheba alone. Bathsheba appears, looking for Troy, and Boldwood is overcome by rage and grief when he overhears how intimate they have become. When Bathsheba has gone he offers to give Troy the money if he will redeem Bathsheba's honour by marrying her at once. Troy shows Boldwood the announcement of his marriage to Bathsheba in Bath and derisively flings the money back at him. Boldwood threatens to punish him and spends the night walking the hills alone.

NOTES AND GLOSSARY:

carpet-bag:	a travelling bag, originally made of carpet

surrogate:	the bishop's deputy; able to grant a licence for marriage without banns
inst.:	of the current month
B.A.:	Bachelor of Arts
M.D.:	Doctor of Medicine. (Troy's mother was married to a poor medical man 'and soon after an infant was born' (Chapter 15), the implication of this being that Edward Troy was not really Troy's father)
Fort meeting Feeble:	forte is the part of a sword blade from the hilt to the middle (the strongest part); foible is the part from the middle to the point (the weakest)
Satan:	Satan was another name for the Devil or Lucifer ('light-bringer' – first among the angels until he rebelled; in the Bible, Revelations 12:9; 20:2, and Isaiah 14:12). Compare Chapter 2. Troy is continuously given devilish associations, and metaphors of light are used for him
Shade ... Acheron:	the shades (souls) of the dead were supposed, by the ancients, to wander on the shores of Acheron (one of the rivers of the underworld) until they could be ferried across

---

Chapter 35: At an Upper Window

The next morning Troy speaks to Oak and Coggan from an upper window of their mistress's house and they gather that Bathsheba has married him. In his distress Oak foresees the long repentance which will ensue from this hasty deed and puts a good face on it for Bathsheba's sake. They pass Boldwood whose whole demeanour, by contrast to Oak's, is expressive of appalling grief and terrible sorrow within himself.

NOTES AND GLOSSARY:
Oak and Boldwood are clearly juxtaposed here in their disappointment. We are not to think of Oak's love as weaker than Boldwood's, but that his concern is really less for himself than for Bathsheba's present and future happiness. Equally, he is quite incapable of thinking ill of her honour, as Boldwood in the previous chapter had done; Oak 'had instantly decided' that Bathsheba and Sergeant Troy were married.

hapeth:	half-pennyworth
half-a-crown:	the old half-crown was worth $12\frac{1}{2}$ new pence
'Troublehouse':	troublemaker

Chapter 36: Wealth in Jeopardy – The Revel

It is the end of August and Troy, now in charge of the farm, is giving the harvest party in the old barn. Oak senses a storm coming and tries to warn Troy of the danger to the uncovered ricks. Troy ignores the warning and orders brandy to augment the cider being drunk, dismissing the women from the revel. When Oak returns to the barn he finds all the men in a drunken sleep, and has to embark alone on covering the ricks.

NOTES AND GLOSSARY:

Just as time for Troy may be told by the artefacts of clocks (Chapter 16) and watches (Chapter 26) while Oak calculates by the unalterable and natural stars (Chapters 2 and 6), so Oak is able to learn from nature here while Troy carouses in ignorance. Oak judges the storm and rain from those closest to nature: sheep, rooks, horses, spiders, toad and slugs. He knows that their instinct will be right.

Her Most Gracious Majesty: Queen Victoria

St Vitus's dances: St Vitus is the saint invoked in cases of epilepsy and one of the diseases affecting the nervous system is named after him; Hardy is using the terminology of illness to describe the musician

DD: in music, the D below Middle D

ath'art: athwart; here, across

show the white feather: show cowardice (a white feather in a game-bird's tail indicates bad breeding)

the Great Mother: Mother Nature, who was anciently known as Cybele and as Ceres by the Romans

furze: gorse

a vandyked lace collar: a collar in which the lace design falls away into long points, in the manner of collars depicted in portraits by the Flemish artist Vandyke (1599–1641)

thirty quarters: a quarter is 28 pounds or 12.7 kilograms

l: £1, a pound sterling

palimpsest: a manuscript from which the original writing has been erased to make room for new

legend: here, an inscription or motto

thatching-beetle: a heavy mallet used for driving in stakes

rick-stick: a tool for combing the straw straight

spars: u-shaped willow rods used to pin the thatch in place

medium: a person who claims to be able to reveal to others the result of extra-sensory perception; a medium would speak in a trance

draw-latching: lazily sneaking in late

Chapter 37: The Storm – The Two Together

Oak works on at covering the ricks in the storm, and is joined by Bathsheba. The storm is tremendous, belittling humanity and its concerns, and endangering the two workers. Wishing Oak to know the truth of her behaviour, since she values his judgement (although not always liking it), Bathsheba explains the circumstances of her visit to Bath: that she was alone and suddenly worried about scandal, that Troy had spoken of a more beautiful woman and that she married him from 'jealousy and distraction'.

NOTES AND GLOSSARY:
The description of the storm is truly dramatic. In the previous chapter Hardy describes the clouds as rising as if by mechanical means, and the final flash of lightning he compares to the Mediaeval German *Totentanz* – a dramatic representation of the universality of death. He gives us vivid colours: blue, green, red, white, and the almost artificial effect of the lightning, throwing deep shadows like a spotlight. The thunder is like a shout, or the strokes of a gong. Where his descriptions are often consciously picturesque, here he makes use of all the theatrical devices.

clog at one eye:	the end of the chain would have been passed through a fixed tethering ring as far as the 'clog' (probably a larger ring attached to one link or 'eye') and then attached to the horse's headcollar
majolica:	Italian pottery with particularly bright glazed decoration
dance of death:	see note on *Totentanz* above
Hinnom:	compare with the 'Tophet' of Chapter 26
zephyr:	a light breeze

Chapter 38: Rain – One Solitary meets another

Oak is still working, now in a downpour, when the revellers emerge from the barn next morning. Returning home he meets Boldwood and learns that the farmer had overlooked the protection of his own ricks and that most of them will be ruined. In trying to avert the mockery of the parish by asserting that he was never engaged to Bathsheba, he does in fact reveal to Oak the bitter depths of his grief.

NOTES AND GLOSSARY:
His infatuation with Bathsheba has paralysed all care of practical matters in Boldwood's mind. Contrast is again drawn with Oak who is clear-sighted over her and whose judgement is not warped by his love.

Flaxman's group ... Mercury: John Flaxman (1755–1826) was an
English sculptor and draftsman of the neo-classic
school. This reference is to one of his illustrations of
the *Odyssey*, 'Mercury conducting the souls of the
suitors to the Infernal Region'. (They were the
suitors of Odysseus's wife, Penelope, and were
killed when her husband returned)

He prepared a gourd ... better to die than to live: an adaptation of the
Bible, Jonah 4:6–8

Chapter 39: Coming Home – A Cry

It is now October and Bathsheba and Troy are returning home from
Casterbridge market one Saturday. Bathsheba upbraids him sadly for
wasting money at races and he replies that she has lost all her pluck and
boldness. They pass Fanny on the road (Bathsheba does not know who
it is) and she swoons on seeing Troy. He sends Bathsheba on ahead and
then arranges to meet Fanny in Casterbridge two days later. He refuses
to tell Bathsheba who the girl was.

NOTES AND GLOSSARY:
Hardy is constantly drawing parallels between his characters. Two
chapters earlier Oak rescued a toad (whose behaviour was useful
evidence to him of the storm). Here Troy, whose horse is equally useful
to him, idly cuts at its ear with a whip to amuse himself.

In Chapter 4 Bathsheba told Oak that she needed someone to tame
her. From her 'flash of indignation' here we may learn that she is not
really tamed by Troy, for all her meekness. Each seems trapped by the
other; Bathsheba is clearly fearful of his selfish folly, he depends on her
for money. The glamour of the relationship has faded and the
practicalities of marriage (in which money may play a large part) are
clearly dividing them.

gig-gentry:	those of sufficient standing and means to own a gig (Chapter 4)
booths:	temporary canvas shelters
cutting:	an excavation of the hillside to take the road
Clk:	a sound of encouragement to the horse

Chapter 40: On Casterbridge Highway

Fanny is finding the three miles to Casterbridge Union-house almost
beyond her strength. She struggles forward and finally arrives by leaning
her weight on a large and friendly dog which mysteriously appears
beside her. The dog is stoned away.

NOTES AND GLOSSARY:
The dog is strangely Christlike: sad, benevolent, homeless, an aid to the friendless, bearing a burden, a shadow on the road (compare the Journey to Emmaus in the Bible, Luke 24:15) and finally rejected (albeit not by Fanny). Hardy probably did not intend this significance, however. In its homelessness the dog is more likely to represent another aspect of the natural world which those with the right qualities can make use of (one thinks particularly of Oak). Fanny thinks of it as embodying aspects of night.

copsewood:	ash and hazel trees (particularly) are cut hard back every few years (coppiced) and the new shoots later cut for making baskets, hurdles, etc. Such an area of trees is a 'copse'
faggoting:	binding cut branches into bundles (faggots)
Jacquet Droz:	a Swiss clockmaker and mechanic (1721–90); his chief work was a writing automaton
flats:	low-lying and often swampy ground
Juggernaut:	the eighth incarnation of the Hindu god Vishnu; its idol was pulled in procession and pilgrims supposedly threw themselves under the wheels of its giant cart. It has come to stand for any huge and remorseless force which ignores the interests of those in its way
guard-stone:	a large stone set at the base of the parapet to protect it from damage
eight hundred yards:	731 metres
threw her idea into figure:	gave her imaginings a concrete form; that is, saw the benevolent aspect of night embodied in the dog
Pleiads:	compare Chapter 2
borough:	town

Chapter 41: Suspicion – Fanny is sent for

Bathsheba and Troy quarrel that weekend; their niggling over his request for money becomes a bitter statement of mutual regret at their marriage, after Bathsheba notices a golden lock of another woman's hair which Troy has been keeping. Her jealousy arises partly from his attachment to the woman and also partly from envy of her beauty. Too late she looks into her own nature, remembering how lightly she valued her maiden freedom and recalling that she sacrificed this freedom in her anxiety for Troy. (Compare the reasons she gives Oak in Chapter 37). On Monday, news is brought that Fanny is dead, and Bathsheba sends

Poorgrass (another of her farmworkers) to bring the body to Weatherbury. By enquiry Bathsheba discovers that Fanny has done much travelling, that her lover was in Troy's regiment, and that her hair was golden.

NOTES AND GLOSSARY:

Hardy tells us that Troy would have succumbed to Bathsheba's beauty had she not been his wife. The reader recalls the account of Bathsheba's own father (Chapter 8) who could only find his wife attractive by pretending he was not married to her. Bathsheba's dependence on Troy, manifested in her beseeching tone, indicates that some of her independent spirit is curbed. For him, as with all rakes, the fascination of a relationship lies in the sport and competition of courtship, not in the co-operation of marriage. He no longer cares to flatter her although he still tries to deceive.

It is ironical that it was Boldwood's threats against Troy which stimulated Bathsheba's rash decision to marry; by now we have been given several reasons for her hasty action.

Bathsheba rightly suspects that she is being kept in ignorance about Fanny. She is well on the way to discovering who Fanny's lover was, but she does not yet realise how significant is the manner of Fanny's death.

non lucendo:	discovery from contraries. (The phrase is *lucus a non lucendo* – the word 'lucus', a grove, is reputed to have been derived from 'lucere', to shine, because a grove is the contrary of shining; 'grove' from 'not shining')
Diana:	Roman goddess of the night and the moon; chaste and averse to marriage. Hardy's comment reinforces his symbolic use of light and darkness in the novel. Troy is a man of light and daytime scenes, Oak a man of darkness; Bathsheba is clearly married to the wrong man (see Chapter 8, 'Night had always been the time at which he saw Bathsheba most vividly')
use nor principal:	here, no part of her at all. (Use is the interest earned by a capital sum of money – the principal)
neshness:	fragility
limber:	frail
candle-snoff:	a candle being extinguished (snuffed)
laurustinus:	an evergreen shrub, flowering in the winter
boy's love:	lad's love or southernwood; an aromatic shrub
Board of Guardians:	the committee which supervised the Union Workhouse and saw that paupers should be cared for and, finally, buried

seampstering:	sewing
handy:	near to
name a hent:	drop a hint, mention

Chapter 42: Joseph and his Burden – Buck's Head

Poorgrass collects Fanny's coffin from the Union-house that afternoon. A sea-mist swirls in upon him and, to revive his spirits, he stops at the Buck's Head Inn on the way home. Oak finds him there much later, still talking with Coggan and Clark and too drunk to drive the cart which Oak takes home instead. Since it is too late for the funeral that evening, Bathsheba orders the coffin to be brought into the house for the night. Without her seeing, and to spare her pain, Oak erases the words 'and child' from beside Fanny's name on the coffin.

NOTES AND GLOSSARY:

Oak foresees the pain gathering for Bathsheba as it becomes increasingly evident that she will find out that Troy was Fanny's lover and that she died giving birth to his child. Although he tries to delay her discovery he feels powerless to forestall the circumstances by which it will come about. This is yet another example of the way in which Oak makes the best of what fate offers.

Traitor's Gate:	the gate opening onto the river Thames by which traitors were admitted to the Tower of London
Alms-house:	compare Chapter 16. Almsmen lived in houses erected by charity
'Malbrook':	*Malbrouk s'en va-t-en guerre* was the first line of an old French nursery song; the tune became popular all over Europe
fustian:	a coarse, dark cotton cloth
plate:	a piece of metal with the name inscribed on it
certificate of registry:	the document certifying that the time and cause of death have been registered
the grim Leveller:	death, which levels all to the same state
meridian:	here, the busiest
stage-coach:	horse-drawn coach running regularly between two places
dew-bit:	a snack taken before the first work of the morning
parish boards:	a coffin provided by the charity of the parish
bell shilling:	a shilling was worth five new pence and was paid for the church bell to be tolled at a funeral
grave half-crown:	the sum paid for the grave (compare Chapter 35)
smoky house:	hell; see Tophet, Chapter 26
whop and slap at:	tackle with energy

chapel-member:	a member of a nonconformist church; Clark considers them to be particularly pious
barley-corn:	ale made from barley-corn
meetinger:	one who attends the chapel (or meeting-house)
skit:	a restive horse
turn king's evidence:	to give evidence at a trial against an accomplice in crime
taties:	potatoes
tracts:	religious pamphlets
horning:	trumpeting
King Noah:	Noah was not a king, but he was commanded to take two of each beast onto the Ark. Compare Chapter 2
Genesis:	the first Book of the Bible
the Eleventh:	the Eleventh Dragoon Guards

Chapter 43: Fanny's Revenge

Lonely and miserable, Bathsheba waits up for Troy that night. Liddy repeats to her a rumour concerning the contents of Fanny's coffin and, feeling in need of a lesson in patience and suspension of judgement, Bathsheba seeks Oak out, recognising that his power of endurance springs from his unselfishness. She observes him through his cottage window and, sensing the great difference between his acceptance of his lot and her rebelliousness, is too proud to seek his help. She returns home and, desperate to know the truth, opens the coffin to find Fanny and her child within. Bathsheba quiets the tumult of vindictive feelings for Fanny but when Troy returns she sees his remorse, his genuine affection for Fanny and is herself repudiated by him. Her despair and indignation master her and she rushes out into the dark.

NOTES AND GLOSSARY:
Hardy draws a distinction between Oak, who, in praying, can 'make a truce with trouble' (seek to avert or mitigate the course of events) and Bathsheba, who has to follow to their end the events she has set in motion. But it is chance which has brought Fanny to Bathsheba's house and, having opened the coffin, Bathsheba is conscious of the horrid irony of her position. It is not until this point that she is able to learn from Oak; 'Gabriel had prayed; so would she'.

The scene by the coffin is highly melodramatic: it is macabre; emotion is raw and basic (anger, jealousy, remorse); words and actions are violent; moral positions are ostensibly clear – the seduced woman destroyed, the jealous wife, the remorseful rake. Since we know the background of the event and characters, however, we know the complex chain of chance circumstances which has brought these sufferers together.

Esther . . . Vashti:	The Book of Esther in the Bible recounts how King Ahasuerus put aside his wife Vashti, who was not prepared to appear as an entertainment for his guests, and took the beautiful Esther instead
lumber-closet:	a little room for storing disused household goods
Mosaic law:	the merciless law by which punishment is exacted in accordance with the crime: 'Eye for eye, tooth for tooth . . . Burning for burning, wound for wound, stripe for stripe' (see the Bible, Exodus 21:24–5). Hardy's 'strife' must be a misreading of 'stripe' (a whiplash)
Tetelestai:	(transliterated) Greek for 'It is finished'. The last words of Christ from the Cross (see the Bible, John 19:30)

Chapter 44: Under a Tree – Reaction

Bathsheba passes the night beside a swampy hollow and in the morning is awakened to the healthy, natural, ordinary world of the early morning, with Liddy coming to find her. She returns to the farm and, with youth and hope reasserting themselves, moves into an attic room to be out of Troy's way. But he does not appear and as evening falls she hears that a grand new tombstone is being erected in the churchyard.

NOTES AND GLOSSARY:
This hollow amid the dying ferns, surrounded by the glistening blades of iris leaves, recalls the hollow where Troy demonstrated his sword-drill to Bathsheba. But this hollow is swampy and dotted with fungi, rotting leaves and dead trees. In describing it Hardy uses the colours of death and decay – red, yellow, brown; and adjectives of pestilence and malignancy – poisonous, evil, clammy, oozing. The difference between these hollows matches the swift and inevitable decay of her misguided relationship with Troy. The sword-drill is again recalled as Bathsheba bitterly comments that the miseries of a runaway wife are worse than the inflictions of one who stays on, despised – 'Stand your ground, and be cut to pieces'.

'like ghosts from an enchanter fleeing':	from P. B. Shelley's (1792–1822) 'Ode to the West Wind'; he is speaking of leaves driven before the wind
flag:	the flag iris; it has long, pointed leaves which Hardy calls 'blades'
psalter:	the Book of Psalms

collect: a short prayer from the Anglican Book of Common Prayer, often appropriated to be read at a particular season or date. The boy is learning the prayer as part of his school homework

stump bedstead: a bedstead with the four upright posts removed (they would formerly have held a canopy over it)

sampler: a piece of embroidery or tapestry worked by a girl as an example of her proficiency

The Maid's Tragedy, The Mourning Bride, Night Thoughts, The Vanity of Human Wishes: the first two are tragedies containing a broken-hearted maiden. *The Maid's Tragedy* (1619) is by Beaumont (*c.*1584–1616) and Fletcher (1579–1625); *The Mourning Bride* (1697) is by Congreve (1670–1729); *Night Thoughts* (1742–5) by Edward Young (1683–1765) is a lengthy poem (some 10,000 lines) on religion and morality. The title of Dr Johnson's poem (1749) is self-explanatory

Love in a Village, The Maid of the Mill, Doctor Syntax, The Spectator: the first two of 1762 and 1765 are comic operas by Isaac Bickerstaffe (*c.*1735–*c.*1812). William Combe (1741–1823) wrote comic verses to accompany Thomas Rowlandson's (1756–1827) drawings of the adventures of 'Doctor Syntax' (published in 1809). *The Spectator*, founded in 1711 by Joseph Addison (1672–1719) and Richard Steele (1672–1729), was a periodical containing the witty 'de Coverley' papers

Prisoners' base: a game in which two parties of players each occupy an area (or base) and try to capture those of the opposite side who leave their base

stocks: a wooden frame with holes for the feet in which petty offenders used to be confined for public humiliation

---

Chapter 45: Troy's Romanticism

In vain Troy had waited for Fanny in Casterbridge with Bathsheba's money that Monday morning, as arranged. Angry because she had failed to appear, as on their wedding day (Chapter 16), he had gone to Budmouth races and then returned home to the confrontation with Bathsheba over Fanny's coffin. The next morning (when Bathsheba is waking in the swampy hollow) he goes to Casterbridge and spends the money on a fine tomb for Fanny. In the evening he returns to Weatherbury and covers her grave with flowering plants, finally resting from the rain in the church porch.

NOTES AND GLOSSARY:

Hardy comments on the unexpected course the day takes for Troy, and how difficult it is to circumscribe events which seem leagued together against one. (There have already been several instances of how Oak's strength lies in the way he can make the best of what fate offers.)

tiring-women:	women employed to dress another
lichen:	a dry, fungus-like plant which can grow on stones
crocketed:	carved with ornamentation of curled leaves or buds
medallions:	decorative panels
flying:	here, flaking or crumbling
sexton:	one who takes care of the church and churchyard and who also may be the gravedigger
picotees:	a kind of carnation

Chapter 46: The Gurgoyle: its Doings

In the heavy rain that night a gurgoyle (or gargoyle) (the carving of a grotesque face designed to drain water from the church roof) spouts a flood of water over Fanny's grave, washing away all Troy's little plants. Feeling his good intentions spurned by Providence, Troy departs from Weatherbury in the morning. Bathsheba and Oak go independently to look at the grave and, meeting there, repair the damage caused by the water-spout.

NOTES AND GLOSSARY:

Troy has discovered that matters do not always necessarily 'right themselves . . . and wind up well' and to live in that belief was to live in an illusion. He does not try to make the best of the way a chance fall of water has ruined the grave, any more than of the way a chance combination of circumstances has brought the final ruin of his marriage.

By contrast, Oak tidies the mess the water has caused on the grave and Bathsheba, who is learning from him now, helps by replanting the flowers.

parapet:	the low wall surrounding the roof-top of the tower
griffin:	a fabulous creature with an eagle's head and wings and a lion's body. Gothic architecture often incorporated these hideous carvings; perhaps to symbolise the grotesque nature of the sins of the world outside the church
seventy feet:	21 metres
duckshot:	pellets of a suitably heavy weight for shooting duck
plinth:	the projecting part of the wall immediately above the ground

Ruysdael:	Jacob van Ruysdael (?1628–82) chiefly a landscape painter, of forests, waterfalls, shore and mountain scenes
Hobbema:	Meindert Hobbema (1638–1709), another Dutch landscape painter
'He that is accursed . . . still':	possibly echoes the Bible, Galatians 1: 8–9
churchwardens:	elected lay representatives of the parish who provide assistance to the vicar

---

Chapter 47: Adventures by the Shore

Troy arrives at the coast in the afternoon and, simply intending a refreshing bathe, is swept out to sea by a strong current. He is rescued by the crew of a brig.

NOTES AND GLOSSARY:
Since the reader knows that Troy and Boldwood strike fire from each other it is necessary, in order for the Boldwood plot to be re-established, for Troy to disappear for a while. Hardy wishes this plot to develop with the protagonists, but not the reader, in ignorance of the truth.

Pacific . . . Balboa's gaze:	Vasco Nuñez de Balboa (1475–1517), a Spanish explorer and the first European to sight the Pacific Ocean (1513)
pillars of Hercules:	the name given by the ancients to the mountains at the western entrance to the Mediterranean; Abyla (in Africa) and Calpe (Gibraltar)
Gonzalo:	Hardy refers to the first scene of Shakespeare's *The Tempest*; during the storm and shipwreck Gonzalo cries, 'I would fain die a dry death'
en papillon:	butterfly stroke; Troy's arms would have gained some rest from the movement through the air
brig:	a two-masted, square-rigged sailing ship

Chapter 48: Doubts arise – Doubts linger

Days pass, but Bathsheba looks to the future in a spirit of hopeless indifference, certain that Troy will return and that they will be evicted from the farm in poverty; that the fatal effects of her mistake are inevitable. At market next Saturday she hears that Troy is drowned and, although she disbelieves it, she swoons into Boldwood's arms. She returns home alone, still disbelieving the news.

NOTES AND GLOSSARY:
In the last paragraphs of this chapter we see what Bathsheba has

learned: she realises that there may be a deception about Troy's death, 'how the apparent might differ from the real', and she also keeps Fanny's hair in a spirit of generosity.

agent to the estate:	Bathsheba is a tenant farmer; the owner would have had an agent to oversee the running of his property
meet:	here, satisfy
rent-day:	payment of rent would have fallen due four times a year
burghers:	citizens (compare Chapter 40)
aldermanship:	the position of authority next to that of the mayor of an English borough council
portico:	an imposing porch supported by columns
coastguardsman:	one appointed by the Admiralty to police a length of coastline
phaeton:	a light, four-wheeled open carriage drawn by two horses

---

Chapter 49: Oak's Advancement – A Great Hope

Winter comes and Bathsheba runs the farm in a spirit of apathy, having promoted Oak to bailiff. Boldwood's farm is suffering neglect and Oak is invited to superintend it as well. Boldwood has hopes again of winning Bathsheba and at haymaking he questions Liddy, discovering that Bathsheba would be free to marry seven years from Troy's disappearance.

NOTES AND GLOSSARY:
Boldwood's hopes are founded on something other than winning Bathsheba's love. He hopes that she will be more considerate now and will still feel remorse for her prank and also that an engagement between them could be suggested as a 'friendly business-like compact'. His idea of an 'intangible, ethereal courtship' of six years is very different from the way she was won by Troy, and will be won by Oak.

the poet's story:	Hardy refers to 'The Statue and the Bust', a poem by Robert Browning (1812–89). A pair of lovers allow wordly considerations to hinder fruition of their love such that they finally place an inanimate statue and bust in their windows to do their enamoured gazing for them. When their bodies die their spirits can only ponder hopelessly, 'What a gift life was, ages ago'. Browning is being ironical; the lovers made no use of the 'gift' as Bathsheba has
cob:	a strong little horse

phantom of delight: Hardy is using Wordsworth's (1770–1850) poem 'She Was a Phantom of Delight' (1804). The first stanza describes a girl with 'eyes as stars of Twilight fair; Like Twilight's, too, her dusky hair . . . a dancing Shape'. The 'second poetical phase' (and stanza) describes her as 'A Creature not too bright or good/For human nature's daily food'. The third stanza – a development in Bathsheba yet to come – describes a woman of 'reason firm [and] temperate will, Endurance, foresight, strength and skill . . . And yet a Spirit still . . .'. This paragraph clearly indicates that we should follow Wordsworth's poem in understanding Bathsheba's development

Jacob . . . Rachel: the Bible, Genesis 29 recounts how Jacob served his uncle Laban for seven years in order to win Rachel for his wife. But Laban married him to his elder daughter Leah and Jacob had to serve another seven years for the younger

---

Chapter 50: The Sheep Fair – Troy touches his Wife's Hand

It is autumn and sheep are being assembled for the annual sale at Greenhill; Oak has taken the flocks of Bathsheba and Boldwood. Among the attractions is a great tent in which the ride of Turpin to York is to be enacted – by Troy. He has been in America and, returning that summer but being loth to face an unpleasant reception at Weatherbury, has fallen in with a travelling circus. Bathsheba watches the performance but does not recognise Troy although her former bailiff, Pennyways, does. He gives Bathsheba a note, telling her that her husband is there, but Troy manages to snatch it from her while she is talking to Boldwood.

NOTES AND GLOSSARY:
It is consistent that Troy, the dissembler, should be able to act a part, and the role of Turpin – an attractive and adventurous villain – is appropriate although there is really little glamour in Troy's sordid affairs. Hardy reminds the reader of Troy's earlier role by the spontaneity with which 'devil' and 'Satan' spring to his lips as oaths.

Nijni Novgorod: a city in central Russia in which an extended summer fair was held annually

statute number: fairs were held on a certain number of days by royal charter

Southdowns, Wessex, Oxfordshire, Leicesters, Cotswolds, Exmoors: breeds of sheep from Midland and south-western areas of England

Royal Hippodrome: a theatre for various stage entertainments

Turpin's Ride ... Black Bess: Dick Turpin (1706–39), thief, smuggler and highwayman, accidentally shot his partner, Tom King, and was finally hanged at York. In legend and fiction he is the hero of a ride from London to York on Black Bess in order to establish an alibi; this legendary ride became the subject of plays and circus acts

ruffen: ruffian

a reed ... wind: 'What went ye out into the wilderness to see? A reed shaken with the wind?' (the Bible, Matthew 11:7)

cheesewring: a press for squeezing the whey from the curds in cheese-making

jumping-jack: a cardboard figure which pops out of a box when the lid is opened

sixpence: half an old shilling; two and a half new pence

Roads: here, stretches of water outside harbour where ships can ride at anchor

read the articles: subscribed to the rules of the ship when joining her crew

Liverpool: city on the west Midlands coast of England, formerly the main port for transatlantic crossings

odd man: odd job man (we are told what these jobs are in Chapter 10)

Rembrandt: Rembrandt van Rijn (1606–69), Dutch painter famous for his rendering of light and shadow (*chiaroscuro*)

'lining': Troy was probably making wrinkles on his face by drawing an oily wire across it

---

Chapter 51: Bathsheba talks with her Outrider

Boldwood escorts Bathsheba home that night and speaks to her of re-marriage. His conjectures (Chapter 49) as to her reception of him prove right; she pities him and is still remorseful, finally agreeing to give him an answer at Christmas. As the time approaches she grows more anxious and finally speaks to Oak, telling him – without vanity – that she thinks Boldwood will go mad if she refuses him. Oak's comment is that the real sin would lie in marrying a man she did not love; Bathsheba feels a greater sin would lie in making no reparation for Boldwood's hurt. She is piqued that Oak does not mention his own love for her.

NOTES AND GLOSSARY:

Boldwood does not really seem to be considering Bathsheba's happiness; he speaks of an agreement which will make him happy and pursues the subject even to the point of frightening her. Knowing that Troy is alive, the reader can see the irony of the situation Hardy is building up for Boldwood.

Bathsheba and Oak express different values in assessing her dilemma. For Oak the sin would lie in making a positive move towards creating much greater unhappiness – marriage without love. For Bathsheba the sin would lie in leaving Boldwood unhappy. Oak has the greater wisdom (although he also has an interest in her); there is little chance of happiness for the couple married with a sense of fear, compulsion, remorse, pity and self-sacrifice on one side, and selfish infatuation on the other. The 'real sin' for both, though, is not a social or legal matter (concerned with propriety or with the law concerning her supposed widowhood) but a matter of human happiness.

Chapter 52: Converging Courses

I It is Christmas Eve and Boldwood's household is preparing a party, although the whole concept of such festivity is alien to his home and nature.
II Bathsheba is reluctantly preparing for the party.
III Boldwood is also dressing and talking to Oak. He is desperately anxious to know whether Bathsheba will keep her promise to accept him.
IV Still jealous, and bearing a grudge towards Bathsheba, Pennyways is keeping Troy (who has left the circus) supplied with information about Bathsheba, Boldwood and the evening's party.
V Bathsheba, anxious not to look too fine and attractive, is ready to leave for the party.
VI Boldwood offers Oak a greater share in the farm management; partly on account of Oak's disappointed love.
VII Muffled in a large cloak, Troy himself is ready dressed for the party – going to claim Bathsheba and the material benefits she can provide him with.

NOTES AND GLOSSARY:
Hardy is giving us a swift succession of parallel vignettes expressing the hopes and fears of the four protagonists as they move together.

Boldwood thinks that Bathsheba's reluctance to accept him is on legal or religious grounds; he is so desperate for the fulfilment of his own happiness that he does not consider hers. He feels in the shadow of trouble but is anxious and yet calmed as he contemplates his future happiness.

Although he shudders with a frightening premonition, Troy is thinking selfishly and confidently about his own material gain, advised by the self-interested villain Pennyways.

In contrast to Pennyways with Troy, Oak subjugates his own interest as he advises Boldwood, although he advises him not to be too confident that all will fall out as he hopes.

Both Troy and Boldwood are really regarding Bathsheba as a possession. She clearly sees the joylessness of her future, her mood being echoed by her black dress and in the seriousness of her tone to Liddy.

Shadrach, Meshach and Abednego: companions of Daniel who were unharmed after being thrown into the burning fiery furnace by King Nebuchadnezzar for refusing to worship his statue (see the Bible, Daniel 3)

ayless: always

lammocken: lounging and slouching

gwine: going

scram: puny

wringdown: the wringing of juice from the apples

plimmed: here, rose. Pennyways is obviously attracted to Bathsheba so that her disdain hurts and angers him the more

cheese: the mass of crushed apples (also pomace or 'pommy')

strawmote: a hollow piece of straw

scroff: scruff, that is, litter or refuse

Juno: the Roman equivalent of the Greek goddess Hera. Her husband, Jupiter or Zeus, found her very self-willed and difficult to manage

Noachian: of the time of Noah; hence, very old fashioned

long-headed: wise

Alonzo the Brave: hero of a ballad by M. G. Lewis (1775–1818), his hideous skeleton claims his fickle bride ('The Fair Imogine') at the feast celebrating her marriage to another

---

Chapter 53: Concurritur – Horae Momento

The farmworkers have heard the rumour of Troy's appearance in Casterbridge and are unsure whether to go into the party to announce it. They repair instead to the Malthouse where they see Troy eavesdropping on Oak and the maltster discussing the party and Boldwood's infatuation. They return to the party but do not get their message to Bathsheba. The party has been hanging fire and Bathsheba is preparing to leave when Boldwood finds her alone. Under his persistent pressure she finally agrees to marry after six years and to wear his ring for the evening. As she is leaving Troy enters and claims her, to her horror.

Boldwood snatches a gun from the wall and shoots Troy. He is prevented from killing himself and so walks out into the night.

NOTES AND GLOSSARY:
Boldwood tells Bathsheba that she is beautiful now, when she is too changed to be moved by praise any more. Although he tries to adopt the reasoning of a 'business compact' with Bathsheba and to force the practical matters of a promise and a date from her, the tone of his persuasion does not allow her to make a reasonable reply. He uses the argument of her debt and the pressure of unanswerable imperatives: 'give your word', 'Say the words . . . say them', 'Promise yourself', 'Be gracious', 'wear it tonight', until Bathsheba is 'beaten into non-resistance'. Troy's imperatives are equally clear: 'Come home with me', 'Come, madam'. In different ways and by regarding her as a possession each has broken – not tamed – her independent spirit; 'her mind was . . . deprived of light'.

Troy has an eye for melodramatic effect; his appearance now electrifies the scene as it had done over Fanny's coffin. We already know him as an actor but here he has entered on a scene whose course, because of Boldwood's instability, cannot be a predictable chain of events – Troy cannot 'enter his old groove' (Chapter 50).

Concurritur – Horae Momento: 'Battle is joined – in a moment of time' ('comes speedy death or joyful victory'); from Horace, *Satires*, Bk. I, Ode i. The Roman poet Quintus Horatius Flaccus (65–8BC) is best known for his *Odes*, his critical treatise *Ars Poetica* and his satires

thik: that

gutta serena: amaurosis; a kind of blindness in which the appearance of the eye is not changed, the optic nerve or brain being damaged or diseased

---

Chapter 54: After the Shock

Boldwood walks straight to Casterbridge and gives himself up at the gaol. Meanwhile, in Boldwood's hall, Bathsheba orders Oak to ride to Casterbridge for a surgeon. When the surgeon arrives he finds that Bathsheba has had Troy's body removed to her home and has, alone, prepared it for the grave. After collapsing from the strain she passes the night in wretched self-recrimination.

NOTES AND GLOSSARY:
From the earlier petty vanity and girlish trifling and after her period of apathy and suffering, Bathsheba is being raised by Hardy to a new level

of maturity. He portrays her power of cool decision and endurance, 'She was of the stuff of which great men's mothers are made' and he likens her to Melpomene, the muse of tragedy.

stoic: here, a person of great self-control and fortitude (from the Stoic school of philosophy, founded in Athens *c.*308BC)

Chapter 55: The March Following – 'Bathsheba Boldwood'

Three months later Boldwood's judges are observed on their way to Casterbridge. Meanwhile, evidence of the madness which Oak and Bathsheba had suspected in him is found at his farm. He had been storing away women's clothes and jewellery, packaged and labelled 'Bathsheba Boldwood'. Oak returns from Casterbridge with the news that Boldwood is sentenced to death. A petition is formed, representing his crime as the result of madness and, literally at the eleventh hour, news is brought that the sentence has been commuted to life-imprisonment.

NOTES AND GLOSSARY:
Here the reader is told that Oak had suspected madness in Boldwood earlier (there is a hint of this in Chapter 35) but that he does not think that Boldwood was deranged when he shot Troy. Bathsheba certainly feared it and it is a question which should be raised in the discussion of Boldwood's character.

javelin-men: men bearing pikes or spears as a bodyguard for the judge arriving at the assizes (court sessions held periodically for the trial of criminal cases)
Circuit: the area within which a judge will travel to assizes
Home Secretary: the government minister in charge of the country's internal affairs
Decalogue: the Ten Commandments (compare Chapter 26)
'First dead ... yode': From *Marmion*, a long poem by Sir Walter Scott (1771–1832) about the perfidious Lord Marmion and the battle of Flodden

Chapter 56: Beauty in Loneliness – After All

It is August and Bathsheba has been almost a recluse for many months. One evening she enters the churchyard and hears the choir practising a hymn which concerns the humility and repentance of one previously ruled by pride. She allows herself to be moved to tears by the hymn. Oak finds her there and announces his intention of leaving England in the spring. As autumn passes he is clearly avoiding her company, and by Christmas Bathsheba is more nearly affected by her neglect than by remembrance of the events of the previous year. His letter of resignation signals to her her loss of his love and, feeling aggrieved, wounded and desolate, she goes to his cottage. There she discovers that his coldness had been only to preserve her good name and that he loves her still. She agrees to marry him.

NOTES AND GLOSSARY:
'Bathsheba revived with the spring' – the pastoral background and the rhythm of the passing seasons must not be ignored in assessing the novel. From this chapter the reader can learn how far Bathsheba has been changed by events. She is bewildered now at the prospect of managing the farm alone; she cares deeply what others think about her, and it is she who is now, voluntarily, in the position of supplicant.

'Lead, kindly Light': this, with the next two quotations, is from J. H. Newman's (1801–90) hymn written in 1833

'all a-sheenen': from 'Woak Hill' by William Barnes (1801–86), the Dorset dialect poet

mentor: an experienced and trusted adviser

'many waters . . . drown': 'Many waters cannot quench love, neither can the floods drown it' (the Bible, The Song of Solomon 8:7)

Chapter 57: A Foggy Night and Morning – Conclusion

Oak and Bathsheba are married quietly some time later, the marriage being cheerfully acclaimed by the farmworkers.

NOTES AND GLOSSARY:
Hardy is able to convince us of the appropriateness of this happy ending for several reasons. Firstly, of those whose destruction might have marred a happy effect: Fanny was lightly sketched and died much earlier; Troy was a villain whose intentions were to further his own material ends at the expense of others' happiness; and Boldwood was increasingly unbalanced in his infatuation which, in its way, was equally selfish and destructive. Secondly (and the matter needs further examination) we are to understand that Bathsheba is tamed, not radically altered perhaps, and sufficiently wise now to create happiness for herself and others. Thirdly, Hardy creates an atmosphere of harmony: by the comradeship between Oak and Bathsheba, by the foggy weather which seems to run day and evening together, and by the actual music of celebration from the farmworkers' band.

church-hatch: the double gate into the churchyard

'Went up the hill side . . .': from 'Patty Morgan the Milkmaid's Story', in *The Ingoldsby Legends* (1840) by R. H. Barham (1788–1845)

'As though a rose . . .': from *The Eve of St Agnes* written in 1819 by John Keats

serpent: a now obsolete wind instrument about 2½ metres long, with several bends and covered with leather

hautboy: the earlier name for the oboe

Marlborough: John Churchill, 1st Duke of Marlborough (1650–1722), a very successful English military commander

'Ephraim . . . alone': from the Bible, Hosea 4:17. Poorgrass is wrong again; the novel is ending on a note of stability and optimism

Part 3

Commentary

Introduction

> 'I find more bitter than death the woman, whose heart is snares and nets ... whoso pleaseth God shall escape from her; but the sinner shall be taken by her'.
>
> (Ecclesiastes 7:26)

Oak repeats the first words of this passage from Ecclesiastes inwardly after he thinks that Bathsheba has been trifling with him and is about to marry Boldwood (Chapter 22). Hardy tempers the anger of it, however: 'This was mere exclamation – the froth of the storm'. Nevertheless the quotation from Ecclesiastes does form a good introduction to the subject of the novel, albeit one which must be tempered as Hardy himself has tempered it.

Oak suffers hurt and disappointment from Bathsheba's irresponsible and often ignorant behaviour. But he is a man who possesses the qualities of patient fortitude and unselfishness which enable him sometimes to transform adverse circumstances, always to endure them. By contrast Troy and Boldwood (in a sense both are 'sinners') are destroyed. As for Bathsheba, Hardy is at pains to illustrate and explain her complex nature – her heart is not intentionally 'snares and nets' to trap and destroy the men around her – and she does attain greater wisdom and humanity.

In assessing the novel, then, the reader needs to examine these characters, asking certain questions about them. What qualities does Oak possess which enable him to survive disaster? Why are Troy and Boldwood destroyed? How much does Bathsheba learn from adversity and how far does she change? What does the setting contribute?

In addition you should consider the way in which the story is treated; style should be a reinforcement of meaning, not mere embellishment. Here specific passages should illustrate Hardy's modes, but an examination of the use of allusion to paintings and to other literary works, and of imagery would be fruitful too.

Finally you can extrapolate the themes which emerge, possibly finding them of wider application than the outline of the story might initially suggest.

Characters

Oak

His surname is the first clue to his character; English oak is renowned for its strength and durability. But his Christian name should not be ignored either. A study of the novel's symbolic structures will reveal the continual juxtaposition of dark and light, Oak and Troy; and within this structure Gabriel emerges as the good angel of God, opposed to the satanic Lucifer.

The tone of Hardy's initial description of him is affectionately comic; he is unwordly, slightly muddled, solid and unpretentious. But 'thoughtful people' (and the tone changes) find him modest, rational and openminded. Hereafter we see him in action and learn both from what he does and thinks as well as from Hardy's own comments as author.

One theme which will emerge is the power individuals hold over their circumstances and what they derive from them. Oak's strength here is obvious. His sheep are destroyed by a disastrous combination of events, but we are told that his strength of character is confirmed by this happening; it leaves him with a 'dignified calm' and an 'indifference to fate' which is the basis of sublimity (Chapter 6). In other matters – ones which materially affect Bathsheba – he is able to avert or mitigate disaster: he extinguishes her fire (Chapter 6), cures her sheep (Chapter 21) and covers her ricks (Chapter 37). He achieves these things by his courage, endurance and good sense, as well as by sympathy with and understanding of the natural world in which he lives.

He has the humanity of the good shepherd; he lives with his lambing ewes and knows the stresses of the new-born lambs. In addition he understands nature's tokens of the coming storm (Chapter 36) and regulates his life by the movement of the stars (Chapter 2). But his appreciation is not wholly utilitarian: 'he stood still after looking at the sky as a useful instrument, and regarded it in an appreciative spirit, as a work of art superlatively beautiful' (Chapter 2).

For all his sympathy with the natural world, however, Oak betrays a lack of tact in his treatment of people. Examined baldly, tact is the compromise which intelligent and sensitive people may sometimes have to make with their sense of honesty. Tact does not have to be the lying flattery of Troy, although it may not absolutely express one's true feelings. Hardy tells us that Oak's qualities will not grant him success with Bathsheba – 'his humility, and a superfluous moiety of honesty' (Chapter 4). We see this clearly as he admits that marrying her would not be wise and again when, 'torturing honesty to her own advantage', she asks his opinion of her conduct towards Boldwood (Chapter 20). It is ironical that she asks him because she counts on his ' disinterestedness of opinion' but is angry 'because the lecturer saw her in the cold morning light of open-shuttered disillusion.' As her predicament becomes more pitiful so Oak learns to treat her with greater sympathy, however, and to temper his strict honesty with humanity. He erases the chalked words 'and child' from Fanny's coffin 'in a last attempt to save Bathsheba from ... immediate anguish' but with a troubled sense of his own powerlessness to counteract the ironical circumstances accumulating for her (Chapter 42). Towards Boldwood he behaves with absolute generosity although he speaks his mind as he warns the farmer of women's fickleness, 'Her meaning may be good; but there – she's young yet' (Chapter 52).

With Troy the matter is different. Oak justifiably suspects his nature and motives and has every cause for antagonism. Coggan perceives a source of disastrous confrontation if Oak is honest, and advises hypocrisy, 'say "Friend" outwardly, though you say "Troublehouse" within' (Chapter 35). In the next chapter Oak's treatment of Troy is remote but civil, and thereafter Hardy keeps them apart.

Bathsheba perceives that Oak's strength is derived from his unselfishness, 'among the multitude of interests by which he was surrounded, those which affected his personal well-being were not the most absorbing and important in his eyes' (Chapter 43). Indifference to fate can only arise from this sort of unselfishness; but his self-effacement nearly ends in losing him Bathsheba. So concerned is he for the preservation of her good name and so apparently set on his vow at the end of Chapter 4 ('Then I'll ask you no more') that he nearly withdraws from her life. In her 'hunger for pity and sympathy' it is Bathsheba who finally seeks him out as he had forced her to do once before over the sick sheep. Their courtship is concluded with the 'good-fellowship' which Oak, but not Bathsheba, had understood as necessary as early as Chapter 4, 'And at home by the fire, whenever you look up, there I shall be – and whenever I look up, there will be you'.

Troy

We are introduced to Troy via Fanny although our knowledge of him is initially limited. The Notes to Chapter 15 explain why we should suspect her judgement of him, and in Chapter 16 we have our suspicions confirmed as he rejects her in a spirit of callous pride and with a selfish sense of hurt dignity.

After Troy's impudent flattery of Bathsheba in the fir plantation (Chapter 24) a whole chapter is devoted to an analysis of him. What Hardy actually says may at times appear complicated but he is not, in fact, describing a very complex character. The reader is constantly aware, in the novel, of Hardy's distrust of absolutes; as an author he is conscious of the way in which moral qualities fade and merge, of the complicated origin and mixture of emotion; and that this blurring and intermingling is often apparent in nature, too. With Troy, however, the case is different. He lacks the subtle refinement of spiritual feelings and the qualities he does possess are 'separated by mutual consent' (Chapter 25). Thus he is a man of intelligence and determination but is 'without the power to combine them' and consequently his intelligence is wasted on trivial matters and his determination employed unprofitably. This really is tied up with Hardy's earlier explanation that Troy is a man of present concerns – he is neither able nor willing to look forward and assess consequences; he is 'the erratic child of impulse' (Chapter 26). This is also why he can be an unscrupulous liar to women and why he is so good an actor; he has no sense of responsibility for his actions. To reinforce his acting ability Hardy always gives him daylight scenes or ones which are brilliantly lit – 'His sudden appearance was to darkness what the sound of a trumpet is to silence' (Chapter 24).

The trivial employment of his intelligence, regardless of consequences, can be observed in his flattery of Bathsheba (Chapters 24 and 26) and his unprofitable use of courage and skill in hiving her bees and the sword-exercise (Chapters 27 and 28). Equally, although he certainly knows the extent of Boldwood's infatuation, he gives no imaginative thought to consequences as he prepares to join the Christmas party: 'I must go and find her out at once – O yes, I see that' (Chapter 52).

His reform is a weak and temporary affair. He chooses flowers for Fanny's grave as a means of adjourning his grief and after they are washed away he has to face the fact that matters do not always 'right themselves at some proper date and wind up well' (Chapter 46). He has no moral strength to continue the reform in the face of adverse fate: 'He threw up the cards and foreswore his game for that time and always'.

Although he may seem to be happy and successful, he is a vain dissembler who wastes his intelligence and perverts his will-power, who gives no imaginative thought to consequences and can profit nothing from his mistakes; hence he is bound for disillusionment and disaster. The disaster occurs when Troy meddles in the unbalanced passion of Boldwood.

Boldwood

To an outsider Boldwood is marked by the pre-eminent characteristic of dignity (Chapter 12) and certainly he is desperately concerned about the way his infatuation must seem to others. Bathsheba is pained to observe how love has deprived him of this 'chief component' (Chapter 23). Later he expresses to her his feeling that the whole world is sneering, 'the very hills and sky seem to laugh at me till I blush shamefully for my folly' (Chapter 31) and to Oak that he must be 'a joke about the parish' (Chapter 38).

This concern with outward dignity and reserve arises because Boldwood's inner nature is so sensitive; it is a protective shell against the world whose mockery he fears. Hardy describes a man whose emotions are held in a fine balance – 'His equilibrium disturbed, he was in extremity at once' (Chapter 18) and whose nature is 'a hotbed of tropic intensity'.

He is also a man naturally disposed to melancholy; before his party he is cheerful but 'almost sad again with the sense that all of it is passing away' (Chapter 52).

Once his equilibrium is disturbed and his judgement distorted by infatuation, his introspective mind occupies itself with morbid assessments of his own folly and idealisation of Bathsheba. This leaves no room for the practical matters of farm management which increases the sense of folly. Winning Bathsheba will mean possession of the physical beauty he observes in Chapter 17, and as he describes his envisaged marriage state it is clear that Bathsheba would be a possession to him, with no activities and employments of her own – 'you shall never have so much as to look out of doors at haymaking time'. To possess her also means relief from his gnawing sense of indignity. This introspective nature becomes wholly selfish as Boldwood presses his suit by a form of blackmail on one whom acceptance will clearly make unhappy.

Oak does not think that Boldwood was really out of his mind when he shot Troy (Chapter 55) and certainly the idea was in Boldwood's head as early as Chapter 34. On the other hand Bathsheba expresses fear for his sanity (Chapter 51); Troy wonders if there had ever been insanity in his family (Chapter 35); and certainly the collection of garments labelled with Bathsheba's name is evidence of an unwholesome preoccupation with her. As the shot is fired Boldwood is without the 'rule' which regulates instinct – the same rule which regulates Troy's sword-drill and keeps it from simple mayhem (Chapter 28). Hardy anticipates the derangement as soon as Bathsheba's valentine arrives, 'the large red seal became as a blot of blood on the retina of his eye' (Chapter 14).

Bathsheba

If Boldwood's passionate nature is only controlled by a vulnerable reserve, Troy, by contrast, is a child of impulse and spontaneity: 'his embellishments [are] upon the very surface' (Chapter 29). Neither possesses a true moral principle for control and guidance. Bathsheba, however, is not static as they are; this 'fair product of Nature' (Chapter 1) with 'an impulsive nature under a deliberative aspect' (Chapter 20) comes to speak of the 'rash acts of [her] past life' asserting that she does 'want and long to be discreet' (Chapter 51). In this she needs guidance.

The episode of the looking-glass in the first chapter is presented as an idle action: it would be 'rash to assert that intention had any part' in it at all. Equally, the valentine to Boldwood is sent in an idle and unreflecting spirit, without any of the intention which Boldwood assumes must be there. In explaining Bathsheba's love for Troy, Hardy describes it as being really the same sort of irrational drifting; 'she felt her impulses to be pleasanter guides than her discretion . . . Her culpability lay in her making no attempt to control feeling by subtle and careful inquiry into consequences' (Chapter 29). We know her capable of making this inquiry since she is 'a woman who frequently appealed to her understanding for deliverance from her whims' (Chapter 20) and this is why the sending of the card and the eloping with Troy *are* culpable.

At the end of the book we are perhaps less convinced that this impulsive nature has undergone transformation than that she has now acquired the wisdom and humility to accept Oak's correction. She has always known the value of his advice and has always been enraged or at least irritated by his air of disinterestedness. At the grinding he tells her he has ceased to think of marrying her (Chapter 20); speaking of Troy he aggravates her by 'letting his wish to marry her be eclipsed by his wish to do her good' (Chapter 29); and after Troy's 'drowning' when she asks his advice 'there existed at this moment a little pang of disappointment . . . Oak had not wished her free that he might marry her himself' (Chapter 51). She has come to regard 'the possession of hopeless love from Gabriel' as an 'inalienable right for life' and on these earlier occasions her vanity is wounded by his apparent independence.

She is impulsive, then, but she is also vain, and this is indicated too by the episode of the looking-glass. Vanity is an essentially selfish quality and one which makes the possessor peculiarly vulnerable to those with clearer sight. It is because she is vain that Bathsheba wishes to conquer the reserved farmer who ignores her presence in the cornmarket: 'it was faintly depressing that the most dignified and valuable man in the parish should withold his eyes' (Chapter 13). If it makes her self-centred, her vanity also opens her to the flattery of Troy. Her reason tells her that he is dissembling and forbids her to listen, but her vanity longs to hear more and prompts her to admit that she enjoys it. She captivates Boldwood and capitulates to Troy wholly blind to the possible consequences of her actions.

Although we may not be convinced that her impulsiveness has been magically transformed, we do gather that her vanity is tamed. She is anxious to appear plain at the Christmas Ball (Chapter 52) and Boldwood's praise of her beauty 'had not much effect now' (Chapter 53). In Chapter 56 the loss of Oak appears less as the loss of an admiring lover than of a supporting friend – 'He who had believed in her and argued on her side', with whom she had had 'the only true friendship she had ever known', 'she was bewildered . . . by the prospect of having to rely on her resources again'.

Hardy is at pains to indicate that there is no absolutely simple solution to Bathsheba's nature, that she is a woman of fine feeling and strong character who nevertheless makes two rash and disastrous mistakes. She is genuinely and deeply distressed by the consequence of the valentine – 'I am wicked to have made you suffer so' she says to Boldwood (Chapter 19), and later she is pained by the change in him (Chapter 23) though her conquest is 'not without a fearful joy'. She is also prepared to pay a highly uncongenial penalty for her thoughtless prank. She suffers, too, for the hasty marriage to Troy because she does actually love him and her happiness with him is threatened by a threefold irony. He still loves Fanny (he tells Boldwood so and we see it demonstrated over the coffin); Bathsheba's affection is not reciprocated by him – for Troy, finally, 'A ceremony before a priest doesn't make a marriage'. And Troy regards Fanny as morally his wife. When these facts are brought home to her Bathsheba suffers in the throes of chaotic emotion: 'she had sighed for her self-completeness then, and now she cried aloud against the severance of the union she had deplored'. Waiting in the swampy hollow next morning she revives as the natural world awakes around her just as, after the final calamity and her period of apathy and indifference, she 'revived with the Spring' (Chapter 56).

Whether she has completed in herself all the attributes of Wordsworth's 'Phantom of Delight' (see Notes to Chapter 49) is arguable. Certainly she does end by demonstrating an inner strength and fortitude; 'she was of the stuff of which great men's mothers are made' (Chapter 54) and, with the 'kindly light' of Oak to guide her, has the means towards greater control and reasonability. Because it has been a romance 'growing up in the interstices of a mass of hard prosaic reality' (Chapter 56), their love has a spiritual quality ('they spoke very little') which transcends normal pleasurable passion and which 'many waters cannot quench, nor the floods drown.'

The setting – the farmworkers

Apart from the specific actions of two or three, the farmworkers have a threefold function in the novel. They act like the chorus of a Greek tragedy, commenting on the main characters but taking little part in the plot; they serve to create the atmosphere which is an integral part of the novel; and they are the main source of its humour.

In Chapter 6 we gather that Bathsheba's vanity is a general topic of conversation locally and from Chapter 8 we learn something of her background from gossip in the malthouse. Particularly discussed is her father's excitement by the thought of sinning ('his will was to do right . . . but his heart didn't chime in') and his subsequent reform. The same sort of conflict between reason and impulse is apparent in Bathsheba. Her pride and vanity are further discussed in Chapter 15, although Henery Fray's criticism springs largely from his disappointed wish for the bailiff's job and his own small-mindedness; 'Bathsheba invariably provoked the criticism of individuals like Henery Fray. Her emblazoned fault was to be too pronounced in her objections and not sufficiently overt in her likings' (Chapter 22). Chapter 33 is devoted to Cain Ball's account of Bathsheba and Troy in Bath by which Oak is prepared for her return as a married woman. In Chapter 53 the men are not sure whether they should, at last, involve themselves in the action by telling Bathsheba that Troy has returned. They delay, wondering whether it is really their business, and by the time Laban goes to find Bathsheba it is too late and they cannot alter the course of events. As they discuss her it becomes clear that for all her mistakes, they admire her: 'she was no otherwise than a girl . . . and how could she tell what the man was made of? . . . she's hot and hasty, but she's a brave girl who'll never tell a lie . . . there's nothing underhand wi' her.'

Similarly, at the end, they appear with their music, not to bring about the happy conclusion, but to celebrate it joyfully.

As the title of the novel and numerous references within make clear, Hardy is concerned with a steady and unsophisticated rural community. He speaks of the 'mercurial dash' of 'men of towns' (Chapter 2) and of the 'refined modesty' of which 'townspeople . . . have no notion whatever' (Chapter 4). In Chapter 18 he describes the unison of rural springtime 'in comparison with which the powerful tugs of cranes and pulleys in a noisy city are but pigmy efforts', and in Chapter 22 he speaks of the immutability of Weatherbury 'in comparison with cities.' For Hardy 'God was palpably present in the country, and the devil had gone with the world to town' (Chapter 22).

The chorus serves to reinforce this sense of wholesome timelessness. They are people for whom the uprooting of a tree or alterations to a well are 'stirring' (Chapter 15). They live by the rhythms of the seasons and features within these are marked by the festivals of the Church; ''tis a very queer lambing this year. We shan't have done by Lady Day . . . And last year 'twer all over by Sexajessamine Sunday' (Chapter 15).

Most memorable are Hardy's picturesque vignettes in which men are simply one harmonious aspect of the natural world. The sheep-dipping is prepared for in language of lush fertility; even the farmworkers are dripping wet (Chapter 19). Hardy begins the shearing with an architectural celebration of the barn and its usefulness and timelessness.

Again, the farmworkers are appropriately and harmoniously placed, 'In the background, mellowed by tawny shade, were the women' and the men are simply a metamorphosed part of the manifestations of spring. Similarly, at the oat-harvest, the drone of flies is reciprocated by the sounds of reaping (Chapter 33).

In reinforcing the stability and rhythm of rural Wessex the chorus serves to highlight the main characters: Bathsheba's impulsive instability, the worthlessness of Troy, and the finally unregulated passion of Boldwood. Equally it serves to confirm our understanding of the source of Oak's patience and endurance.

The third prime function which all serve is maintaining the humorous tone of a novel whose ingredients could easily make for a tragic ending. This is achieved largely by the idiosyncrasies of the men; like the rustics of Shakespeare's *A Midsummer Night's Dream* they take themselves very seriously. Jan Coggan and Mark Clark, however, are always ready for a joke, and to restore good humour and mollify anyone if the joke has gone too far.

Henery Fray is a 'man of bitter moods' (Chapter 8) who feels that his abilities have been slighted and that he should have replaced the thieving bailiff Pennyways. In Chapter 22 he recounts how he spoke to Bathsheba but not 'so plain that she could understand my meaning, so I could lay it on all the stronger'. His sense of injury is his recurring theme and after Bathsheba waves aside his officious aid in Chapter 10 he will not easily believe good of this 'froward piece'.

Such overt self-assurance is not to be found in Joseph Poorgrass. He is shy and fearful, but nevertheless has a good opinion of his own piety which is really nearer superstition. He self-consciously makes a virtue of timidity, and his inability to hold liquor he calls his affliction of a 'multiplying eye'. He also has the hypocritical habit of couching his 'profound' statements in biblical language and then pretending they are worthless, 'I don't like dwelling upon it, [his 'reflectious way'] for my few words are my few words, and not much' (Chapter 55). He is also one of the few rustic characters materially affecting the action. He is too superstitious and has too much fondness for drink to have been sent alone for Fanny's coffin. Once at the Buck's Head Inn he keeps intending to leave and each time is easily persuaded to stay; and finally the coffin is taken into Bathsheba's house for the night with traumatic consequences for her (Chapter 42). The stages of his drunkenness are written with great control – he does not become incoherent, simply muddled, nor any more violent than a petulant rabbit.

Coggan and Liddy serve a fourth function, each in a different manner. For all the 'private glimmer in his eye' (Chapter 8) Coggan is quite a good confidant for Oak He wisely advises caution over Troy (Chapter 35), aids him in the chase after Bathsheba (Chapter 32) and finally helps with the wedding preparations (Chapter 57). Liddy, on the other hand, is a disastrous confidante for Bathsheba. She encourages her mistress in the folly of the valentine, and is anxious, through fear, to say whatever Bathsheba wishes to hear (Chapter 30). But it is also Liddy who most importantly represents the goodness of human kindness as she seeks Bathsheba out after the row over Fanny's coffin (Chapter 44).

Hardy's style

Perhaps the most straightforward way of tackling the difficult subject of style is to divide the subject under the headings of description, reflection, and dialogue, in order to make an initial assessment. Finally, an examination of allusion and imagery will be helpful.

Description

Hardy's technique lies in appealing to certain of the reader's senses so that the scene may be re-created in the imagination. He does this by the use of particularly vivid and evocative words. Where movement is involved the words are mainly verbs, and where all is still they are adjectives.

In Chapter 2, for instance, the wind 'smote the wood and floundered through it'. It grumbles and gushes, simmers and boils, ferrets and rattles. It is movement for the ear; the grasses rub and rake and brush, the trees wail, chant and sob. The tumult of the scene is enhanced because these are human activities, but they are out of control and chaotic. It anticipates the tumultuous emotion to follow later in the novel. By contrast, Chapter 19 begins with the sheep-dipping. Hardy invites us to use our eyes; it is 'a sight to remember long' and the movement of moisture is almost 'observable to the eye'. The adjectives are those of lush fulfilment: the sod is rich and damp, the reeds are swelling and flexible, leaves are new, soft, moist and, for the ear, *three* cuckoos are sounding their notes of peace and reassurance. This Arcadian sweetness and ripeness is suitable for the 'mild sort of apotheosis' Boldwood has made of Bathsheba and for the setting of his first proposal to her.

Hardy achieves his vivid effect by the use of words that are particularly concrete as well as clear and vigorous. In Chapter 11 he describes the onset of winter; 'the retreat of the snakes, the transformation of the ferns, the filling of the pools, the rising of fogs, the embrowning by frost, the collapse of the fungi, and an obliteration by snow.' The process is precise and inevitable. It is also appropriate to a scene which furthers Fanny's disaster. Circumstances transform her too; she fades, collapses, and sinks towards death.

Reflection

In philosophical reflection upon his subject Hardy is not always so clear. He has so complete an awareness of the complexity of things that several dangers confront him: he may become contradictory and inconsistent; he may become incomprehensibly abstract; and he may become verbose.

He avoids the first danger by making his three main male characters fairly straightforward, although they are not oversimplified. Bathsheba is a woman and in Hardy's view she is therefore inevitably inconsistent. He speaks of her 'whims', her 'capricious inconsequence' and her womanly power of believing what is false and being sceptical over truth (Chapter 29), of snubbing constancy and bewailing fickleness (Chapter 24). Any inconsequence in her nature he ascribes to her femininity; 'she had too much understanding to be entirely governed by her womanliness, had too much womanliness to use her understanding to the best advantage' (Chapter 29). Given this sort of inbuilt irrationality the character need never be inconsistent and may thereby appear, in fact, the more human.

In abstract discussion Hardy is sometimes less clear, particularly when widening his discussion of the particular to the universal. In Chapter 25, when describing Troy, he moves to a general statement about the sort of people whose finer feelings are limited by an inability to look forward: 'But limitation of the capacity is never recognised as a loss by the loser therefrom in this attribute moral or aesthetic poverty contrasts plausibly with material, since those who suffer do not mind it, whilst those who mind it soon cease to suffer.' Here Hardy seems so determined to be crisp that he loses clarity. 'Capacity' is having to carry much meaning over from the previous sentences and then 'attribute' is having to assimilate it all. The ellipsis created by excluding 'poverty' following 'material' forces the reader to concentrate on grammar at a crucial point for meaning, while the final phrases actually force the reader to stop and paraphrase in order to follow Hardy's sense. (If a man is not able to experience finer feelings he does not necessarily regard this as a loss and thus it may in fact seem better to be spiritually rather than materially poor. This is because those who put up with spiritual poverty do not mind it, and those who do mind it soon do something to repair it). In so far as much of the novel is descriptive or in dialogue and Hardy's reflections are usually much shorter, the reader is not often confronted with such difficulties.

Verbosity is not a flagrant fault either, but is one which does occur if Hardy is trying to give serious weight to a reflective discussion. The tenth paragraph of Chapter 25 (beginning 'The wondrous power of flattery . . .') is an example of the way in which lengthy or latinate words may lend an air of almost comic pomposity to the passage: perception, corollaries, complemental, aphorisms, catastrophe, tremendous, reflectiveness, co-ordinate, deluging, untenable, perdition, unsought, wringing, aforesaid, indulgence. All Hardy is really saying is that it is likely that there must be an element of truth in the flattery that is to succeed with women and although no-one really knows, some have tried to find out by experiment. The nature and power of flattery is certainly one of the novel's main themes, but Hardy has made this sufficiently clear in action and really does not need this turgid exposition.

Dialogue

Good dialogue should further our knowledge of the characters and impress us with its immediacy and verisimilitude. Explicitly, it reveals the extent and the limitation of the speaker's knowledge, implicitly it may reveal a good deal about his nature.

Chapter 52 presents a series of vignettes in which Bathsheba, Boldwood and Troy speak of hopes and fears to a confidant. Bathsheba fears more trouble: 'I have never been free from trouble since I have lived here'. Her tone to Liddy is subdued and she speaks in short, troubled phrases. Boldwood's manner conveys greater self-confidence; 'I have become the young and hopeful man'; but he is also apprehensive and speaks to Oak 'feverishly' in rhetorical questions and occasionally disjointed sentences. Troy is flippant and off-hand, contemptuous of Pennyways and unreflectingly self-confident. Each is dressing for the party; each is speculating on what the evening will hold; but the dialogue distinguishes three very different people, with different expectations and attitudes.

The farmworkers are mostly revealed in dialogue and certainly the introduction to them is wholly dramatic (Chapter 8). Each is individualised by the way he speaks and is spoken to. Laban Tall is characterised as 'Susan Tall's husband'; his tone is serious and good-natured and he is addressed with cheerful jocularity. The maltster, as befits his years, speaks with an authority to which others defer, but in a generous spirit of keeping him happy, 'It was the unvarying custom in Weatherbury to sink minor differences when the maltster had to be pacified' (Chapter 22). Cain Ball and his choking exasperates the others who are desperate for news from Bath (Chapter 33). Comedy arises from the disparity between Oak's urgent interest in one subject only and the wish by the others to offer a comment of some weight and consequence on other matters.

Chapter 26 contains the second stage of Troy's conquest of Bathsheba. Here he is flattering her, but by devious means, and the dialogue develops into repartee like sword-play. Initially her replies would have dismissed any other man, but Troy always has a brisk answer, such that she is rendered 'absolutely speechless'. His flattery disarms her by its directness and she becomes increasingly unsure of her replies 'because its vigour was overwhelming'. Her questions indicate her uncertainty and also a naive curiosity. As for Troy, we have to be informed that he suddenly speaks in earnest, since recognition of Bathsheba's beauty does not prompt a changed expression from his earlier lies; in fact we are told that he speaks 'mechanically' and that Bathsheba is still half-suspicious. She is left in a state of bewilderment because Troy has here been using the dialogue to disguise himself and conceal his real feelings from her.

Allusion

Hardy aims at stimulating the imagination of the reader as he refers to particular paintings or artists, and at enriching the understanding by the use of other literary works.

By allusions to paintings he generally either creates the effect of tableau or directs our attention to the particular quality of a colour. As Troy and the others emerge from their revel in the barn they are likened to a procession in a particular painting by Flaxman (Chapter 38). We gather well enough that they are dishevelled without the allusion, but the effect is enhanced if the picture is known. After the rain in the churchyard Hardy describes the landscape in terms of 'beauties that arise from the union of water and colour with high lights' in the paintings of Ruysdael and Hobbema (Chapter 46) and the light in the fair-tent as 'intensified into Rembrandt effects' (Chapter 50). The grey of Oak's dog has faded like a Turner water-colour (Chapter 5), Liddy's face has the hue found in seventeenth-century Dutch portrait painters (Chapter 9), while Maryann's is more like a sketch by Poussin (Chapter 22).

Hardy's allusions to works by Shakespeare, Keats, Shelley, Browning, Swift, Cowper, Homer and Ovid serve to illuminate the tiny areas in which they are used, and not a great deal is lost if they are not recognised.

This is not true, however, of Hardy's allusions to Milton's *Paradise Lost*. These he uses to further the theme concerning Bathsheba's loss of innocence and the devilish insinuation of Troy, giving them thereby the wider significance of human weakness and temptation, error, punishment and forgiveness. Wordsworth's poem 'She Was a Phantom of Delight' is also significant, in that Bathsheba's development loosely follows its stanzas.

But the novel is most notable for its continual allusions to the Bible. These are used for illustration, where the result is a semi-absurd bathos which lightens tone – like Gabriel's hut compared with Noah's Ark (Chapter 2) or Boldwood's aloofness compared with the intransigence of Daniel (Chapter 13). Equally, biblical references are nearly always comic when muddled hopelessly by the lovable hypocrite Poorgrass. The use of Ecclesiastes to describe Oak's feelings about Bathsheba is, however, much more serious. It is a book Hardy knew well (he once considered turning it into Spenserian stanzas) and allusion to it does draw our attention to the serious themes of good and evil doing, the incompleteness of our knowledge, and the need for fortitude in the face of chance and time.

Hardy does, of course, make use of other knowledge: of architecture, of the church services, of classical mythology and of rural activities in general. It all lends flavour to the novel, although it can occasionally be more mystifying than illuminating and (as with the architecture) it can be actually annoying where one's imaginative effort is halted by some incomprehensible term.

Imagery

Sometimes Hardy's use of simile and metaphor gives deeper significance to a particular episode, and occasionally he sustains the use of a particular metaphorical idea throughout the novel.

After the destruction of his flock, Oak thinks of Bathsheba as he stands beside a pond – 'over it hung the attenuated skeleton of a chrome-yellow moon . . . the morning star dogging her on the left hand . . . a breeze blew, shaking and elongating the reflection of the moon without breaking it, and turning the image of the star to a phosphoric streak upon the water' (Chapter 5). With the pool glittering 'like a dead man's eye' the whole scene evokes a feeling of exhaustion and collapse. The moon is a 'skeleton' and the word 'dogging' implies threatening and patient pursuit. The whole passage could be regarded as a depressing metaphor for Bathsheba's future relationship with Troy. She, the moon, is not broken by the buffetings she receives from fortune and he, the star ('How art thou fallen from heaven, O Lucifer, son of the morning!') has a short, but dashing, career. The connection of Bathsheba with the moon is made again later by Hardy; 'Diana [the chaste moon-goddess] was the goddess whom Bathsheba instinctively adored' (Chapter 41) and when Bathsheba makes her final visit to Oak he opens 'the door, and the moon shone upon his forehead' (Chapter 56). This metaphor is connected with Hardy's use of light and darkness and will be drawn into the specimen essay answer on this subject (see page 84).

From the sixth paragraph of Chapter 42 Hardy creates a similar atmosphere for the return of Poorgrass with Fanny's coffin. As it approaches, the mist takes the nature of fungus; spongy, rooted, elastic. The clear air becomes like an eye blinded by opacity, and the trees take on human attributes: intent, but indistinct and shadowless like spectres, beaded grey with the mist like old men. The words 'grey' and 'dead' are repeated and the sound of a drop on the coffin only serves to intensify the silence. Here Hardy has endowed the woodland with life only to transform it to the grey stillness of death. The description is appropriate to the action but it serves also to frighten into delay the man who, when lost by night, once spoke to an owl (Chapter 8).

By contrast, in Chapter 6, Hardy begins his description of the rick-fire in the simple terms of colour, shape and sound. But the passage ends with the evocation of devilishness as the fire takes on the Gothic, gargoyle face of evil. As with the doings of the church gargoyle (Chapter 46) there is suddenly a sense that man's efforts are being thwarted by some malign power.

The evil and destructive redness of the flames is associated with an image which Hardy maintains throughout the novel for Troy; that of a man whose whole appearance is of a dazzling red. Bathsheba finds herself hooked to him 'brilliant in brass and scarlet' (Chapter 24) and when she goes to meet him for the sword-drill he is 'a spot of artificial red' in the distance (Chapter 28). Boldwood watches him return to Weatherbury, 'the lamp . . . illuminated a scarlet and gilded form' (Chapter 34) and he keeps a scarlet jacket even as a farmer – he shines 'red and distinct' as Oak looks at the sleeping revellers (Chapter 36) and Hardy is careful to mention the jacket as they all emerge later. But when he dies 'scarcely a single drop of blood' has flowed; his association is with the brilliant redness of hell-fire, not with bloody destruction.

Themes

The discussion of imagery naturally leads to an examination of themes since particular metaphors and similes often recur as part of a sustained idea. A brief analysis of these themes indicates how fuller discussions might develop.

Responsibility

In this rural community responsibilities fall into two categories: the practical responsibilities of each one by which the community survives, and the moral responsibilities by which it is kept stable. Although Oak could be an independent man he freely chooses to add his skills to the Weatherbury community, systematically and effectively. In addition he acts as mentor to Bathsheba and she slowly grows to an awareness of her need for his aid both practically and morally.

Troy is equally independent. The aid he lends with the hay and the bees is simply a convenient gesture. He has chosen not to belong to the community and returns in a spirit of moral irresponsibility to wreak havoc as 'the impersonator of Heaven's persistent irony' towards Boldwood (Chapter 53).

Boldwood's sense of responsibility is demolished by his passion. Practically, his affairs are neglected by his preoccupation with Bathsheba, and finally his moral sense is overturned by the jealous impulse which prompts the murder of Troy.

Bathsheba is also handicapped – by her sex. Although her presence as a farmer in the cornmarket is accepted, it is also 'unquestionably a triumph to her as the maiden' (Chapter 12). As her farming career progresses it becomes clear that she does need practical assistance with farmyard crises: the burning ricks, the sick sheep, the uncovered grain. These call for a strength and skill which she simply does not possess. As mentioned earlier, Hardy views her womanliness as a handicap to her sense of moral responsibility too. She needs the 'kindly light' of Oak as a guide 'amid the encircling gloom' of the final loneliness, desperation and fear brought about by her earlier acts of female irrational wilfulness.

A reader might feel that a spirit of anti-feminism directs Hardy's portrayal of Bathsheba. This would not be just, since he is clear that she is a woman of commendable qualities who makes irresponsible mistakes but who comes to understand her own deficiencies which are made up by the partnership of marriage.

Communication

Much of the plot of the novel springs from the idea that communication between people can, and does, break down.

In their dealings with Bathsheba all three men are less than clear, but for different reasons. We have already seen how Oak may be honest to the point of tactlessness; but he can be silent too. He does not tell Bathsheba that he has found evidence of Troy's lies to her (Chapter 29) and he nearly loses her by refusing to speak further of marriage and by keeping out of her way. Troy uses words to deceive. He lies to Bathsheba until she cannot tell what is true and what is false, and he deliberately misleads Boldwood (Chapter 34). Boldwood's words have the wrong effect; the more he presses his passion on Bathsheba, the more fearful and uncertain she becomes.

The confusion which words may create is reflected in the uncertainty some characters feel over the intentions of others. Bathsheba's whims make her intentions difficult to fathom but 'she was no schemer for marriage' (Chapter 18). Boldwood says to her, 'I took for earnest what you insist was jest, and now this that I pray to be jest you say is awful, wretched earnest' (Chapter 31). Troy deliberately exploits his ability to conceal his intentions: 'he could speak of love and think of dinner; call on the husband to look at the wife; be eager to pay and intend to owe' (Chapter 25).

Untrustworthy words, however, are not the only means of communication; looks are expressive too. Bathsheba's honesty is supported by the readiness with which she blushes. Her face betrays the embarrassment of guilt which might otherwise be concealed. She blushes as she speaks with Oak in the early chapters; at the stare of Boldwood (Chapter 18); and at Troy's appearance in the hayfield (Chapter 25). The state becomes 'little less than chronic' (Chapter 30) with her excitement over Troy's wooing, until finally 'the blood fired in her face' as she paces to and fro beside Fanny's coffin in a spirit of rebellious anger, self-recrimination and broken pride.

Eyes, too, have much to tell. Oak and Bathsheba hardly look at each other as they talk of marriage across the hollybush (Chapter 4). Of Boldwood's anger Hardy writes, 'There are accents in the eye which are not on the tongue . . . Boldwood's look was unanswerable' (Chapter 31). And Troy impudently looks so hard at Bathsheba that she is forced to lower her eyes (Chapter 24). There is truth to be learned from both the direction and the expression of the eyes.

It is significant that Oak and Bathsheba do not, finally, need to speak of their mutual feelings, 'pretty phrases being unnecessary' (Chapter 56). Bathsheba has learned to suspect them and Oak never has been 'able to frame love phrases' (Chapter 4). True communication lies in the instinctive sharing of feeling; one 'would as soon have thought of carrying an odour in a net as attempting to convey the intangibilities of . . . feeling in the coarse meshes of language' (Chapter 3).

Celebration of the natural

We are to understand that what is natural is good. Of the preparations for the party Hardy writes that 'the proceedings were unnatural . . . and therefore not good' (Chapter 52). From time to time and at crucial moments, he gives us a description of unnatural effects in nature; these are the reversal of what one normally expects and occur when fortunes reach a turning point for the worse. As Boldwood meditates by night on the valentine, 'His window admitted only a reflection of [the moon's] rays, and the pale sheen had that reversed direction which snow gives, coming upward and lighting up his ceiling in an unnatural way, casting shadows in strange places, and putting lights where shadows used to be' (Chapter 14). The lantern in Chapter 24 has the same sort of effect: 'It radiated upwards into their faces, and sent over half the plantation gigantic shadows of both man and woman, each dusky shape becoming distorted and mangled upon the tree trunks till it wasted to nothing'.

Nature, nevertheless, provides an indistinctness and lack of complete definition which does not necessarily presage ill, although it may accompany a depressing event. Here sky and land may sometimes merge or the vision become uncertain. In Chapter 31, after Boldwood's fury, the sky is described in terms of land; nature is inverted, 'Above the dark margin of the earth appeared foreshores and promontories of coppery cloud' and in Chapter 42 'the waggon and its load rolled no longer on the horizontal division between clearness and opacity, but were embedded in an elastic body of monotonous pallor throughout.'

The unnaturalness which is 'not good' is embodied in the person of Troy and can be identified by several tokens. Firstly, he is not a character whose elements are mingled; clashes of feeling do not work in him to produce a richer emotion but '[confound] one another, [produce] a neutrality' (Chapter 43). We have been told of his incapacity for finer feelings, and as he moves towards Fanny's coffin it is with the uncomplicated emotions of dismay, sadness and remorse. This deficiency prevents him from feeling any sort of natural charity or real generosity. Secondly, he is presented as a man who will abuse the world by which he lives: making the farmworkers drunk, neglecting the grain-stacks, lashing his horse's ear. Thirdly, Hardy gives us a man who has chosen to leave his natural community and who only returns to make use of it. He is described as a patch of 'artificial' red in Chapter 28 and his mode of life moves him from town to town. He is the child of a Parisienne and an earl, and, although he is a 'natural' son, he is out of place and destructive in the natural world.

Others may be very different, both inextricably complex, and natural, in their emotions and their *modus vivendi*. Bathsheba's tears beside Fanny's coffin are of 'a complicated origin, of a nature indescribable, almost indefinable' (Chapter 43). Later she is described as having lived 'in a state of suspended feeling which was not suspense' and now 'in a mood of quietude which was not precisely peacefulness' (Chapter 49). When Fanny recognises Troy on the Casterbridge road 'Her face was drawn into an expression which had gladness and agony both among its elements' (Chapter 39), and later she is able to cheer the dog while sorrowing in her heart (Chapter 40).

Bathsheba's capacity for natural feeling is great and complex, and this is why she suffers so deeply. But she is also a woman who is quite at home in her rural environment. She can ride as if part of the horse and milk a cow, as well as win the respect of farmers and farmworkers. We see little of Fanny, but she resourcefully makes use of every natural aid in her struggle towards Casterbridge.

Oak is the supreme example of a man living with nature: using but not abusing, benefiting but not pillaging, altering but not destroying. His 'special power, morally, physically and mentally, was static, owing little or nothing to momentum as a rule' (Chapter 2) and this is why he is able to stand apart from 'the madding crowd' with an invulnerable sense of wider forces working together in nature. 'Human shapes, interferences, troubles and joys were all as if they were not, and there seemed to be on the shaded hemisphere of the globe no sentient being save himself' (Chapter 2).

Part 4

Hints for study

Preparation of the text

Preliminary reading

Reading a novel for examination purposes poses its own problems. The text is not conveniently divided into acts and scenes and the composition is not necessarily 'memorable' in the manner of verse. What you must try to do, therefore, is to supply these sort of aids for yourself.

First reading should familiarise you with the subject of the book; both its action (what happens) and its themes (what the action means). Knowing the text well is a prime requisite, learning to deploy this knowledge is largely a matter of practice although there are certain knacks which can help.

Structure

The structure of the plot of *Far from the Madding Crowd* is really based on Bathsheba's activities. The general summary has indicated how divisions may be made although you should be wary of applying them too rigidly; they are indicative of emphasis and are not exclusive.

The novel also has a sub-structure, however, which serves both to create the pastoral setting and, in a symbolic sense, to reinforce the mood of the action. This sub-structure lies in the passing of the seasons. Oak loses his flock, and Bathsheba, in the winter. As summer approaches his material fortunes rise and so do Boldwood's hopes of winning Bathsheba. At the height of summer Troy arrives, but fortunes begin to wane as he woos and wins Bathsheba. As winter approaches Fanny dies, Troy is lost and Bathsheba lives on in a spirit of apathy. Oak still increases his social standing and advantages. Bathsheba revives with the spring and as summer waxes so do Boldwood's renewed hopes of winning her. By the autumn sheep-fair more disaster is brewing; and in the dead of winter Troy is murdered, Boldwood imprisoned, and Bathsheba left in even deeper desolation and despair. With the second spring come new hopes, founded on the prospect of a truly happier and unthreatened future.

In the third place you should consider the detailed movement of the novel between day and night. How many of Oak's scenes are by night, how many of Troy's by day? How many chapters begin with 'later that night' or 'one fine evening' and phrases of that sort? In fact you will find that, of the fifty-seven chapters, almost half (twenty-six) are set by night or in the evening. These aspects of the novel's structure should help to imprint its plot, as well as some of its wider themes, on your mind.

In the second reading you should be ready to note down matters of more detail which are going to be of use in discussion of the novel. It is a good idea to make general headings on several sheets of paper and then to mark the text as you read and to note the page reference and quotation, with your own comments, under the appropriate heading on the paper. The headings should be fairly general and may include more detailed sub-headings, thus:

CHARACTERS: Oak   (*i*)   what the author says
                                     about each.
                Troy
                             (*ii*) what other characters say
                Boldwood   about each.

                Bathsheba
                             (*iii*) the implication for his character
                Fanny   of what each says and does.

                minor
                characters

Number three may appear the hardest, because it is the least explicit, but it is really only a matter of making the same sort of rational and evidenced interpretation that you may make in your 'real life' interpretation of people. Thus Essay 8 (p.87) is asking, among other things, for an assessment of Boldwood's character.

SETTING: interiors   For instance, Oak's hut, the malthouse,
                        Boldwood's house.
            exteriors   For instance, Bathsheba's house or specific
                        scenes (these are multifarious and do not
                        need listing here).

Ask yourself what these descriptions add. You should then find yourself thinking about features of Hardy's style.

STYLE: Here you might examine details of Hardy's way of expressing images and ideas. You may find a passage striking – either because it is particularly vigorous and clear or because it is peculiarly flaccid and obscure. Ask yourself 'Why?' repeatedly. *Why* is the passage describing Bathsheba's awakening in the swampy hollow effective? (Chapter 44). Is it because Hardy is using words that are concrete and colourful:

'beautiful yellow ferns', 'a fulsome, yet magnificent silvery veil', 'the blades . . . glistened in the emerging sun'? Is it also because he uses words which evoke a particular feeling or mood: the 'aspect of the swamp was malignant', 'its moist and poisonous coat', 'their clammy tops . . . their oozing gills', 'red as arterial blood', 'a nursery of pestilences small and great'? Hardy's great strength in natural description lies in looking at things very closely.

THEMES: Although an author may speculate explicitly and philo-sophically on a particular theme (for instance, Hardy on flattery in Chapter 25) he may, equally, leave the reader to arrive at the wider implications of the novel for himself. This you can only do by giving serious and sustained thought to what the action and interests of the novel imply. Any novel which deals at length with the inter-relationships of a group of well-delineated people is inevitably going to draw a great number of serious concerns into consideration.

Much harder to perform – and to describe – is the best way of organising all this material in order to answer a particular question most effectively. The following three specimen essays suggest different, but not exclusive, ways of approaching a topic and organising material for it.

Specimen questions and approaches

(1) What part does Fanny Robin play in the novel?

APPROACH: Here you might ask yourself a series of related questions in order to arrive at what is really required, and set them out in the way suggested below. On what occasions does she appear?

Chapter 7: Oak meets a timid and unnamed girl in the dark outside Weatherbury. 'Her voice was . . . suggestive of romance'; the ironic prefiguring of her wish to go to The Buck's Head; 'a throb of tragic intensity'; 'the penumbra of a very deep sadness'.

Chapter 11: On a wintry night she speaks to Troy through a barracks window. Reversal of roles.

Chapter 15: Contains her happy and optimistic letter to Oak.

Chapter 16: She mistakes churches (but is unnamed).

Chapter 39: She speaks to Troy one evening on the Casterbridge road; she is not named.

Chapter 40: She struggles towards the workhouse. A fox barking 'with the precision of a funeral bell'; 'she had an object in keeping her presence on the road . . . unknown'; 'the panting heap of clothes'.

Chapter 41: She is discussed in Weatherbury. 'She was such a limber maid that 'a could stand no hardship'.

Chapter 42: Fanny's body is brought home. 'She's dead, and no speed of ours will bring her to life'.

Chapter 43: Bathsheba opens the coffin and Troy returns. You must study the effect on Bathsheba of what she finds: she feels uncharitable, listless, weary, mocked by fate, angry. 'Events were so shaped as to chariot her hither in this natural, unobtrusive, yet effectual manner'. Fanny's mean condition has become grand by her dying.

Chapter 45: Troy puts flowers on her tomb. His actions are described, even before they are nullified by the gargoyle, as futile and absurd.

Is hers a major role? No, it is her effect on others that is significant. What part has she in the plot? She serves to bring Bathsheba to complete knowledge of Troy, and thus to separation from him. Does her role have any bearing on themes? Certainly chance and coincidence play a part in her story.

SPECIMEN ANSWER:

At first sight a reader might think that Fanny's role is very small, and certainly it is a curiously negative one. She appears in only five chapters and is anonymous (except as 'Fan' in Chapter 11) in all of them. With one exception these are also night scenes. In three later chapters her corpse is the subject of much discussion and the cause of a turbulent and emotional scene between Troy and Bathsheba. In a further chapter, memory of her affects Troy's doings.

In the first place, then, she serves to introduce a feeling of unease and mystery concerning her future and Troy's character. Oak is aware of the stress she is under (Chapter 7) and we gather this ourselves in Chapter 11 where the timid girl has made all the practical arrangements for the wedding; some great fear must be prompting her resource and effort. All this seems to be resolved, however, when Oak receives her cheerful and optimistic letter in Chapter 15. But then she makes her fatal mistake over the churches and is abandoned by Troy. From his treatment of her we discover his callousness, selfishness and vanity. The mystery surrounding her trouble returns with her secrecy on the Casterbridge road, and the resolution of the 'throb of tragic intensity' is anticipated by the difficulty of her journey and the bleakness of the night.

If, alive, her role was passive, after her death she dominates the thoughts of all; first of Oak and Boldwood who wish to preserve Bathsheba from knowledge of Troy's perfidy; then, erratically, of the local people; then of Bathsheba herself; and finally of Troy.

Most impressive is the gamut of emotions which Bathsheba runs in Chapter 43. She thinks of Fanny without charity and of herself as mocked by fate: 'events were so shaped as to chariot her hither in this natural, unobtrusive, yet effectual manner'. But after Troy appears all her indignant feelings about 'compromised honour, forestalment, eclipse in maternity by another' are 'forgotten in the simple and still strong attachment of wife to husband'. The presence of Fanny's corpse serves to heighten the emotional tension by which both Bathsheba and Troy come to express the truth of their feelings for each other: 'I love you better than she did', 'You are nothing to me – nothing'.

Finally, Troy makes an impulsive gesture of temporary remorse by decorating Fanny's grave. When this effort seems spurned by Providence he gives up such reformation and re-embarks on his wayward and reckless life.

Fanny's role, then, is vital both for the plot – bringing events to a head – and for the aspect of the novel's symbolism which deals with chance and fate. However hard she may try to direct the practical affairs of her life (her marriage, her safety in the workhouse, the second meeting with Troy) circumstances thwart her. Indeed she is finally used as a kind of instrument in the hands of fate. Ironically, 'the panting heap of clothes' achieves 'The one feat alone – that of dying – by which a mean condition could be resolved into a grand one'.

---

(2) Write an essay on Hardy's symbolic use of light and darkness

---

APPROACH: These notes may serve to show how you can marshall ideas and quotations before embarking on the topic.

    (*i*) Hardy's continual use of light effects: the effect of silhouette; for example, Oak's dog and Fanny's dog.

    (*ii*) The nature of light: natural; for example, moon, stars, daylight, etc.; artificial; for example, lamps, flashing material, . . .

    (*iii*) The juxtaposition of Oak and Troy: Oak – natural light; steady, helpful, illuminating; Troy – artificial light; dazzling, blinding, deceiving; Bathsheba 'dazzled by brass and scarlet'.

SPECIMEN ANSWER:

Both as author of a novel with a pastoral setting and as a man interested in paintings, Hardy makes continual use in his descriptions of the effects of light. And where he juxtaposes light and darkness the use becomes more than description and takes on a symbolic importance.

As Fanny struggles towards Casterbridge in Chapter 40 Hardy describes the town light as 'appearing the brighter by its great contrast with the circumscribing darkness'. Conversely, he makes repeated use of the effect of silhouette; dark against light. The result of this is usually to give greater significance to what is silhouetted; the minutiae of individuality are removed and the shape may take on a grandeur or universality that does not necessarily belong to it. Thus Oak's reckless dog stands 'against the sky – dark and motionless as Napoleon at St Helena' (Chapter 5). Here the use creates bathos; later, on the

Casterbridge road, Fanny's canine helper stands 'darkly against the low horizon' and the creature's mysteriousness is heightened as Fanny endows it with the 'sad, solemn and benevolent' qualities of night (Chapter 40).

But more impressive, because sustained and consistent, is the juxtaposition of Oak and Troy; the one illuminating darkness, the other dazzling the sight. Here one is aware of the difference between the natural light of moon and stars, which are steady, consistent and timeless, and the fitful, dazzling and ultimately untrustworthy glimmer of the artificial illumination of lamps, lanterns and bright material.

Oak is named after Gabriel, the 'hero of God' and second archangel who may be contrasted with the rebel Lucifer ('light-bringer'). Many of the chapters in which he appears are set at night, and we see him as a man who regulates his life by the stars and whose work is done as swiftly and easily by night as by day. It is not for nothing that Hardy presents him in titanic struggle with the devilish light of the rick fire, and, later, fighting to save the crops in a dazzling thunderstorm, nor by chance that Bathsheba should be listening to Newman's beautiful hymn as Gabriel appears beside her in the church porch (Chaper 56). (It has been held that by 'kindly light' is meant the inherent, natural sense of goodness pertaining to humankind.)

Troy, on the other hand, is a figure of sunlight, or one illuminated by lamps and lanterns. Chapter 24 presents him as dramatically lit in the fir plantation. But the mangling and distorting of his shadow prefigures ill, just as the unnatural shadows cast by violent lightning in Chapter 37 give a sense of impending violence and disaster, 'a copy of the tall poplar tree on the hill was drawn in black on the wall of the barn' (like gallows). Boldwood sees Troy lit by a carriage lamp before their quarrel (Chapter 34) and Troy works by lamplight on Fanny's grave before abandoning his good efforts: 'the rays from Troy's lantern spread into the two old yews with a strange illuminating power, flickering, as it seemed, up to the black ceiling of cloud above' (Chapter 45). But one chiefly associates him with the *aurora militaris* of Chapter 28 by which Bathsheba 'is enclosed in a firmament of light' by his swordplay, is kissed before he disappears 'almost in a flash, like a brand swiftly waved' and is left feeling 'like one who has sinned a great sin'.

Her sense of judgement is blinded; Boldwood tells her later that she is 'Dazzled by brass and scarlet'. A period of distressed withdrawal follows her mistake, 'Bathsheba drew herself and her future in colours that no reality could match for darkness', (Chapter 48) until finally circumstances and her altered nature bring her back to Oak, 'down she sat, and down sat he, the fire dancing in their faces' (Chapter 56), in a new and permanent security and companionship.

---

(3) How far are chance and coincidence responsible for the events of the novel?

APPROACH: Here you may be able to hinge your answer on a preliminary quotation and to test its significance against the events of the novel.

SPECIMEN ANSWER:

'It is safer to accept any chance that offers itself, and extemporise a procedure to fit it, than to get a good plan matured, and wait for a chance of using it' (Chapter 6).

Oak is waiting vainly for employment at the hiring-fair. With the destruction of his flock he has already had to acquire an indifference to fate, now he learns that it is better to invent some means of coping with what chance provides than waiting for what circumstances offer.

Hardy draws a distinction between those who deliberately choose to be directed by chance or who are at the mercy of the whims of fate, and those who are able to make an effort of will to alter or improve circumstances.

The decision to send the valentine is made by the chance fall of a tossed book, and Bathsheba is culpable because her reason could easily have told her that the action was mistaken. Once it is sent and the consequences begin to dawn on her, she finds there is no escaping from her action and no way of altering circumstances.

The other fatal mistake is made by Fanny, but not wantonly. Once the chance similarity of church names has confused her and lost her her bridegroom, she also discovers that the inexorable chain of disaster cannot be broken, however hard she tries.

Troy does not try. We are told that his force of character wastes itself in useless grooves; and certainly, after Fanny's mistake, he does nothing to alter or circumscribe the chance happening. His activities 'never being based upon any original foundation or direction, they were exercised on whatever object chance might place in their way' (Chapter 25). Temperamentally, he is what Bathsheba wilfully chooses to be, and after chance has thrown them together, chance then accumulates a series of perverse circumstances which they cannot alter or escape from; 'She must tread her giddy distracting measure to its last note, as she had begun it' (Chapter 43).

It is an accumulation of chance happenings which brings Troy and Bathsheba together over Fanny's coffin: if Poorgrass had not been chosen to convey it, it would have arrived in time to be buried; if Oak had not been praying, Bathsheba might have asked him about Fanny. They are chance circumstances, but they are operating on character: Poorgrass's timid susceptibilities, and Bathsheba's rebellious refusal to 'make a truce with trouble' by praying.

Although chance happenings may set an inexorable chain of events in motion, they only cause the destructive events of the novel insofar as they operate on susceptible characters. Just as Troy is moved towards Bathsheba in the first part, so a chance collection of events moves him towards Boldwood at the end and with even greater disaster. In his unbalanced passion, but with his determined character, Boldwood reaches for his gun in a desperate attempt to stop the 'persistent irony' of Heaven towards him.

Oak is not exempt from the operations of chance, but because he is neither wilful (like Bathsheba) nor weak (like Fanny) nor inconsequential (like Troy) nor irrational (like Boldwood), he is able to mitigate or endure adverse events – '"nothing happens that we expect", he added, with the repose of a man whom misfortune had inured rather than subdued' (Chapter 38). He has the unselfish strength and sense of wider purposes which enable him to overcome the hindrances created by 'circumscribing events, which appear as if leagued together to allow no novelties in the way of amelioration' (Chapter 45).

Oak seeks, consequently, to rebuild his fortunes after his sheep have been destroyed by mischance; to save the uncovered ricks from ruin by the savage storm; and to delay Bathsheba's knowledge of the contents of Fanny's coffin, brought to her house by an unfortunate delay. He is able to bring some sort of rational order into the arbitrary and 'heartless' events of nature, and nowhere does Hardy express this more clearly and effectively than in Chapter 2 when, above the windy uproar, 'Suddenly an unexpected series of sounds began to be heard in this place up against the sky. They had a clearness which was to be found nowhere in the wind, and a sequence which was to be found nowhere in Nature. They were the notes of Farmer Oak's flute'.

Further essay topics

(4) Discuss the power of love as it is portrayed in *Far from the Madding Crowd.*

(5) To what extent has Bathsheba altered by the end of the novel?

(6) Discuss the main characteristics of Hardy's style.

(7) Trace the development of Bathsheba's relationship with Oak.

(8) Why did Boldwood shoot Troy?

(9) Discuss the theme of the nature and power of flattery.

(10) Examine Hardy's use of colour, and suggest what this contributes to the novel.

Part 5

Suggestions for further reading

The text

The New Wessex Edition, Macmillan, London, 1975, provides an excellent text for study of *Far from the Madding Crowd*, as well as other work by Hardy.

Other works by Hardy

Novels and collected stories (with date of original publication):
    Desperate Remedies, 1871
    Under the Greenwood Tree, 1872
    A Pair of Blue Eyes, 1873
    Far from the Madding Crowd, 1874
    The Hand of Ethelberta, 1876
    The Return of the Native, 1878
    The Trumpet-Major, 1880
    A Laodicean, 1881
    Two on a Tower, 1882
    The Mayor of Casterbridge, 1886
    The Woodlanders, 1887
    Wessex Tales, 1888
    A Group of Noble Dames, 1891
    Tess of the d'Urbervilles, 1891
    Life's Little Ironies, 1894
    Jude the Obscure, 1896
    The Well-Beloved, 1897

Collections of poems:
    Wessex Poems, 1898
    Poems of the Past and the Present, 1901
    Time's Laughingstocks, 1909
    Satires of Circumstance, 1914
    Moments of Vision, 1917
    Late Lyrics and Earlier, 1922
    Human Shows, 1925
    Winter Words, 1928

Notebooks and letters

HARDY, E. (ED.): *Thomas Hardy's Notebooks*, Hogarth Press, London, 1955.
OREL, H. (ED.): *Thomas Hardy's Personal Writings,* Macmillan, London, 1967.
PURDY, R. L. and MILLGATE, M. (EDS.): *The Collected Letters of Thomas Hardy*, Oxford University Press, Oxford, 1978.

Background

COX, R. G. (ED.): *Thomas Hardy: The Critical Heritage*, Routledge & Kegan Paul, London, 1970.
PINION, F. B.: *A Hardy Companion*, Macmillan, London, 1968.
PURDY, R. L.: *Thomas Hardy: A Bibliographical Study*, Oxford University Press, Oxford, 1954.

Biography

GITTINGS, R.: *Young Thomas Hardy*, Heinemann, London, 1975.
GITTINGS, R.: *The Older Hardy*, Heinemann, London, 1975.
HARDY, F. E.: *The Life of Thomas Hardy, 1840-1928*, Macmillan, London, 1962.

Criticism

The following books contain essays or chapters on *Far from the Madding Crowd.*
BROWN, D.: *Thomas Hardy*, Longman, London, 1954.
CARPENTER, R. C.: *Thomas Hardy*, Twayne, New York, 1964.
GUERARD, A. J.: *Thomas Hardy: The Novels and Stories*, Oxford University Press, Oxford, 1959.
KRAMER, D. (ED.): *Critical Approaches to the Fiction of Thomas Hardy*, Macmillan, London, 1979.
KRAMER, D.: *Thomas Hardy: The Forms of Tragedy*, Macmillan, London, 1975.
MILLGATE, M.: *Thomas Hardy: His Career as a Novelist*, Bodley Head, London, 1971.
MORELL, R.: *Thomas Hardy: The Will and the Way*, University of Malaya Press, Kuala Lumpur, 1965.
STEWART, J. I. M.: *Thomas Hardy: A Critical Biography*, Longman, London, 1971.

The author of these notes

BARBARA MURRAY was educated at the University of St Andrews. After obtaining the degrees of M.A. and B.Phil. there, she completed a Ph.D. thesis at Girton College, Cambridge, on the theory and practice of comic adaptation in the seventeenth and eighteenth centuries. She is now a lecturer at St Andrews University.

York Notes: list of titles

CHINUA ACHEBE
Things Fall Apart

EDWARD ALBEE
Who's Afraid of Virginia Woolf?

MARGARET ATWOOD
The Handmaid's Tale

W. H. AUDEN
Selected Poems

JANE AUSTEN
Emma
Mansfield Park
Northanger Abbey
Persuasion
Pride and Prejudice
Sense and Sensibility

SAMUEL BECKETT
Waiting for Godot

ARNOLD BENNETT
The Card

JOHN BETJEMAN
Selected Poems

WILLIAM BLAKE
Songs of Innocence, Songs of Experience

ROBERT BOLT
A Man For All Seasons

CHARLOTTE BRONTË
Jane Eyre

EMILY BRONTË
Wuthering Heights

BYRON
Selected Poems

GEOFFREY CHAUCER
The Clerk's Tale
The Franklin's Tale
The Knight's Tale
The Merchant's Tale
The Miller's Tale
The Nun's Priest's Tale
The Pardoner's Tale
Prologue to the Canterbury Tales
The Wife of Bath's Tale

SAMUEL TAYLOR COLERIDGE
Selected Poems

JOSEPH CONRAD
Heart of Darkness

DANIEL DEFOE
Moll Flanders
Robinson Crusoe

SHELAGH DELANEY
A Taste of Honey

CHARLES DICKENS
Bleak House
David Copperfield
Great Expectations
Hard Times
Oliver Twist

EMILY DICKINSON
Selected Poems

JOHN DONNE
Selected Poems

DOUGLAS DUNN
Selected Poems

GERALD DURRELL
My Family and Other Animals

GEORGE ELIOT
Middlemarch
The Mill on the Floss
Silas Marner

T. S. ELIOT
Four Quartets
Murder in the Cathedral
Selected Poems
The Waste Land

WILLIAM FAULKNER
The Sound and the Fury

HENRY FIELDING
Joseph Andrews
Tom Jones

F. SCOTT FITZGERALD
The Great Gatsby
Tender is the Night

GUSTAVE FLAUBERT
Madame Bovary

E. M. FORSTER
Howards End
A Passage to India

JOHN FOWLES
The French Lieutenant's Woman

ELIZABETH GASKELL
North and South

WILLIAM GOLDING
Lord of the Flies

GRAHAM GREENE
Brighton Rock
The Heart of the Matter
The Power and the Glory

THOMAS HARDY
Far from the Madding Crowd
Jude the Obscure
The Mayor of Casterbridge
The Return of the Native
Selected Poems
Tess of the D'Urbervilles

L. P. HARTLEY
The Go-Between

NATHANIEL HAWTHORNE
The Scarlet Letter

SEAMUS HEANEY
Selected Poems

ERNEST HEMINGWAY
A Farewell to Arms
The Old Man and the Sea

SUSAN HILL
I'm the King of the Castle

HOMER
The Iliad
The Odyssey

GERARD MANLEY HOPKINS
Selected Poems

TED HUGHES
Selected Poems

ALDOUS HUXLEY
Brave New World

HENRY JAMES
The Portrait of a Lady

BEN JONSON
The Alchemist
Volpone

JAMES JOYCE
Dubliners
A Portrait of the Artist as a Young Man

JOHN KEATS
Selected Poems

PHILIP LARKIN
Selected Poems

D. H. LAWRENCE
The Rainbow
Selected Short Stories
Sons and Lovers
Women in Love

HARPER LEE
To Kill a Mockingbird

LAURIE LEE
Cider with Rosie

CHRISTOPHER MARLOWE
Doctor Faustus

ARTHUR MILLER
The Crucible
Death of a Salesman
A View from the Bridge

JOHN MILTON
Paradise Lost I & II
Paradise Lost IV & IX

SEAN O'CASEY
Juno and the Paycock

GEORGE ORWELL
Animal Farm
Nineteen Eighty-four

JOHN OSBORNE
Look Back in Anger

WILFRED OWEN
Selected Poems

HAROLD PINTER
The Caretaker

SYLVIA PLATH
Selected Works

ALEXANDER POPE
Selected Poems

J. B. PRIESTLEY
An Inspector Calls

WILLIAM SHAKESPEARE
Antony and Cleopatra
As You Like It
Coriolanus
Hamlet
Henry IV Part I
Henry IV Part II
Henry V
Julius Caesar
King Lear
Macbeth
Measure for Measure
The Merchant of Venice
A Midsummer Night's Dream
Much Ado About Nothing
Othello
Richard II
Richard III
Romeo and Juliet
Sonnets
The Taming of the Shrew
The Tempest

Troilus and Cressida
Twelfth Night
The Winter's Tale

GEORGE BERNARD SHAW
Arms and the Man
Pygmalion
Saint Joan

MARY SHELLEY
Frankenstein

PERCY BYSSHE SHELLEY
Selected Poems

RICHARD BRINSLEY SHERIDAN
The Rivals

R. C. SHERRIFF
Journey's End

JOHN STEINBECK
The Grapes of Wrath
Of Mice and Men
The Pearl

TOM STOPPARD
Rosencrantz and Guildenstern are Dead

JONATHAN SWIFT
Gulliver's Travels

JOHN MILLINGTON SYNGE
The Playboy of the Western World

W. M. THACKERAY
Vanity Fair

MARK TWAIN
Huckleberry Finn

VIRGIL
The Aeneid

DEREK WALCOTT
Selected Poems

ALICE WALKER
The Color Purple

JOHN WEBSTER
The Duchess of Malfi

OSCAR WILDE
The Importance of Being Earnest

THORNTON WILDER
Our Town

TENNESSEE WILLIAMS
The Glass Menagerie

VIRGINIA WOOLF
Mrs Dalloway
To the Lighthouse

WILLIAM WORDSWORTH
Selected Poems

W. B. YEATS
Selected Poems

York Handbooks: list of titles

YORK HANDBOOKS form a companion series to York Notes and are designed to meet the wider needs of students of English and related fields. Each volume is a compact study of a given subject area, written by an authority with experience in communicating the essential ideas to students at all levels.